THE DYING BREATH

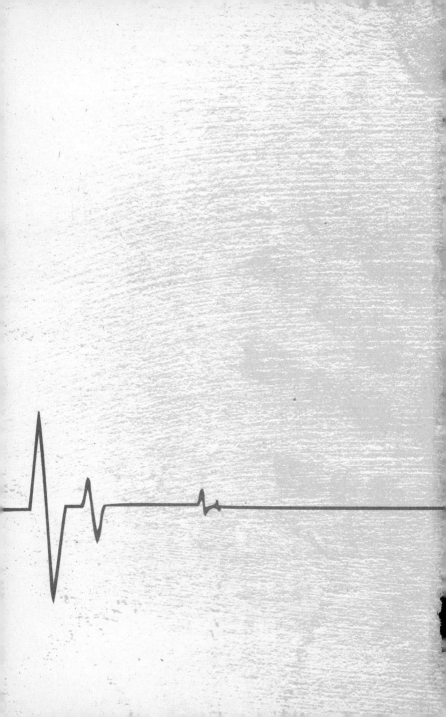

THE DYING BREATH

BREATH

a forensic mystery by
Alane Ferguson

VIKING
An Imprint of Penguin Group (USA) Inc.

VIKING

Published by Penguin Group

Penguin Group (USA) Inc., 345 Hudson Street, New York, New York 10014, U.S.A.

Penguin Group (Canada), 90 Eglinton Avenue East, Suite 700, Toronto, Ontario,
Canada M4P 2Y3 (a division of Pearson Penguin Canada Inc.)

Penguin Books Ltd, 80 Strand, London WC2R 0RL, England

Penguin Ireland, 25 St Stephen's Green, Dublin 2, Ireland
(a division of Penguin Books Ltd)

Penguin Group (Australia), 250 Camberwell Road, Camberwell, Victoria 3124, Australia
(a division of Pearson Australia Group Pty Ltd)

Penguin Books India Pvt Ltd, 11 Community Centre, Panchsheel Park,
New Delhi – 110 017, India

Penguin Group (NZ), 67 Apollo Drive, Rosedale, North Shore 0745,
Auckland, New Zealand (a division of Pearson New Zealand Ltd.)

Penguin Books (South Africa) (Pty) Ltd, 24 Sturdee Avenue, Rosebank, Johannesburg
2196, South Africa

Penguin Books Ltd, Registered Offices: 80 Strand, London WC2R 0RL, England

First published in 2009 by Viking, a member of Penguin Group (USA) Inc.

10   9   8   7   6   5   4   3   2

LIBRARY OF CONGRESS CATALOGING-IN-PUBLICATION DATA
Ferguson, Alane.
The dying breath : a forensic mystery / by Alane Ferguson.
p. cm.
Summary: When her ex-boyfriend starts stalking her, seventeen-year-old Cameryn
must use her knowledge of forensic sciences to protect herself.
ISBN 978-0-670-06314-7 (hardcover)
[1. Stalking—Fiction. 2. Forensic sciences—Fiction. 3. Coroners—Fiction. 4.
Interpersonal relations—Fiction. 5. Mystery and detective stories.] I. Title.
PZ7.F3547Dy 2009
[Fic]—dc22
2009002170

Printed in the U.S.A.   Set in Bookman ITC light   Book design by Jim Hoover

To Brent Safer, who gave me Ireland, and his beautiful wife, Kathy, my true SL!

Chapter One

"THERE'S NO WAY I can let you in that house with the remains," Sheriff Jacobs told Cameryn. A small man, the sheriff leaned his hip against the porch's wooden railing, his expression obscured by the sun's reflection on his glasses. He took a long drag from his cigarette, sending a plume into the frigid February air, then lazily flicked the ashes onto the snow-encrusted bushes below. "Sorry to smoke in front of you—I wouldn't do it 'cept it cuts the smell. There's not another odor in this world like the stench of a decaying human and I, for one, can't stand it." Another drag, and then, "And I'd appreciate it if you stopped rolling your eyes at me, Cameryn Mahoney. I know you're assistant to the coroner, but you're only seventeen and your father, the real coroner, ain't here yet, which means *I'm* the one in charge. We're not breaking in until Pat gets here."

"Except you're not listening. We don't have to break anything!" Cameryn protested.

The sheriff cut her off. "Dream on. Leather Ed keeps this dump locked up tighter than a drum." Jacobs waved his cigarette toward the metal bars that wept trails of orange rust onto the home's weathered siding. "Bars on the windows, deadbolts on the doors, all to protect stuff that isn't even worth stealing. Soon as my deputy gets here he'll bust us in, and then we'll go inside, *together*, to see what's what. Afterwards you can take your pictures of the dead." He pinched the cigarette between his thumb and forefinger, taking a long drag. "You know, I'll never understand why a pretty girl like you . . ." His voice trailed off, but Cameryn no longer listened because her mind was focused on other things.

The answer, she knew, was in the door itself. She peeled off her thick coat and dropped it next to a pile of trash Leather Ed had stacked against the siding, a stack that had grown to a height of almost three feet. Squatting, she examined the dog-door flap, darkened to black from years of grime. Leather Ed owned an emaciated German shepherd that had already been removed by a worried neighbor, a man who had called the police, who had, in turn, called the coroner's office, who'd sent a text to her. Death had its protocol.

Studying the frame around the dog door, Cameryn mentally took its dimensions; then with a tentative swipe she kicked the weathered plastic. The panel swung back and forth like a metronome, revealing a patch of dirty floor and a crumpled edge of a paper plate. Difficult, yes, but she could clear it, with or without Jacobs's consent. She got on her knees and began to back in feet first, her hair falling into her face in a dark curtain. It was a tight fit. As she moved she tried not to picture the filthy linoleum her jeans would scrape against or notice the fresh wave of odor that wound around her like a pungent scarf. The metal lip of the dog door dug into her backside and she was just tilting onto her hip when she felt hands yanking her beneath her armpits. The sheriff pulled her to her feet with so much force she almost cried out.

"Are you *crazy*?" Jacobs's expression was the same one everyone in Silverton wore whenever they looked at her now. Lines of worry, and inside that, real fear. "Your father would skin me alive if I let you out of my sight." His hand sliced through the air as he talked over her protests. "No, Cameryn, not even for a single moment. No, no, *no*!"

"Come on, I only want to go a few feet inside so I can unlock the door—that's all!" she cried. "Let me do my job, Sheriff. I'm not an infant."

"No, what you are is a target." Leaning close, Jacobs

dropped his cigarette onto the porch. With a slow, sure motion, he ground the stub beneath the heel of his boot. "No one knows what's in that house. Probably nothing but the body of the town eccentric. But the fact is, Kyle O'Neil's got you in his crosshairs and right now you're on my watch. I'm not taking any chances." He paused for a moment, for effect, Cameryn guessed, but she wouldn't let him see how his words had hit home. The verbal punch to her heart—she had learned to take the hit without flinching where outsiders could see. She forced her eyes to meet his, which were cold and wintry gray. Raising her chin, she said, "That's ridiculous. Kyle's gone."

"How do you know that?" Jacobs tapped his finger to his temple. "Huh? Use that famous brain of yours. There ain't no body."

"Yes, but—"

"But nothing. I know everyone in town is saying that psycho got lost in those mountains and froze hisself to death, and I hope to the good Lord they're right. Maybe come spring we find his sorry carcass frozen in some creek. But you need to think about this: if that boy had enough smarts to kill his teacher, he's smart enough to keep hisself alive, even in February." He jabbed his forefinger at Cameryn. "Until we find him, I say you're in danger, which means you're staying right here by my side. Understand?"

There was nothing to say. Looking past him, she focused on a hermit thrush perched on the rim of a toppled bird feeder, its claws as fine as thread. It was a trick she'd begun to master, a mental dodge she used when people insisted on pressing themselves into her life: stare at something else, concentrate on the detail of the thing. Let their words pass over like water.

"I'll take your silence as a yes," Jacobs told her. "And now, if you'll excuse me, I'm gonna call my deputy. He shoulda been here by now." Jacobs stomped down the rickety porch steps and turned his back toward her, one finger screwed into his ear while he pressed the phone into the other.

Cameryn was aware of the cold creeping through her too-thin shirt, grateful that it cooled the heat of her frustration. Overhead, above a mountain peak, the palest moon shimmered, a golden coin floating in a blue water sky. In the past, her beloved mountains had felt protective. Now, they'd become walls. Walls that echoed the word that had come to define her.

Target.

It was the perfect word for what she'd become. She was no longer Cameryn Mahoney, senior at Silverton High, straight-A student, science geek, and forensic guru. When she walked the hallways at school whispers followed, marking her new identity: *The Victim. The Hunted. Prey.*

She had almost loved him once. Kyle O'Neil, the boy who, with terrible precision, had tried to kill her. Before the police arrived he'd vanished into the mountains, and Cameryn had believed the FBI when they announced he'd been spotted in Mexico. And yet, as Silverton glittered beneath strings of Christmas lights, Cameryn had received a message on her bedroom computer. *I see you. Come out and play. Move your curtain and look out. By the trees. I'm waiting.*

She'd pulled back her curtain. There, illuminated by moonlight, stood Kyle. Even in the half-light she'd recognized his muscled frame, his square jaw, the yellow hair glinting like dandelion fluff, his legs thick as tree trunks rooted into the ground. His face had been too deep in shadow for her to make out his eyes, but she could see the curve of the mouth. He was smiling.

Kyle raised his hand, touching his heart with his fist before extending his open palm toward her. Horror flooded her as he faded back into a stand of pine. It was only then she realized she was screaming.

And once again Kyle O'Neil had vanished. It was the second time he'd threatened her life. This time, though, the town's reaction had been different. Aware that she'd been twice menaced, Silverton had pulled together for Cameryn's protection, and she felt as though she were an insect caught in a web. It was as if she would suffocate in the silk cocoon of good intentions.

Now she watched as Sheriff Jacobs paced across Leather Ed's yard, his boots cleaving snow. "Yes, Justin, Cammie's with me." He stole a glance at Cameryn before twisting away. "Quit worrying . . . she won't do nothing without my say-so. I've got it under control."

At that moment Cameryn felt something click in her head. *She won't do nothing without my say-so.* Maybe if she took back the power in her life again, people would stop looking at her like the victim she was more conclusively becoming every minute. And she knew exactly what she had to do.

She looked at the door, her nerves tingling. Throwing a quick glance in the sheriff's direction, she backed to the dog door and dropped to her knees again, this time pushing fast, scraping her vertebrae against the metal frame with so much force she knew she would have a bruise down her backbone. She didn't care. Once inside, she rocked back on her knees, exhilarated as she steadied the swinging flap with her hand. For the first time in a long while she'd done something on her own, and the independence was electrifying.

It was dim inside. As Cameryn unfolded herself, she brushed off the front of her jeans, taking a moment to allow her eyes to adjust. The kitchen countertops were piled with plates and paper cups. A coffeepot, so stained the white plastic had turned to sepia, tipped drunkenly on a broken base. Although she'd never been inside the house, Cameryn had waited on Leather Ed many times at the Grand, and the interior of the home was exactly what she expected. A mess.

She drew in a breath and tried not to taste the stench of death that almost overpowered her. So far, Jacobs hadn't sensed her absence, which would give her time to open the door in triumph. *It is better to beg forgiveness than ask permission* was a phrase her friend Lyric had taught her. But when she reached her hand to unlock the deadbolt she realized there was nothing to turn. The face of the brass deadbolt was smooth and flat; a keyhole yawned where the knob should have been. Staring, she tried to compute the dichotomy. How could a bolt need two keys? The outside of a lock demanded a key, but the inside lock should require only a turn of a handle. This side of the deadbolt was blank.

"*Cammie!*" She heard the sheriff curse and the heavy stomp of his boots on the porch. He pounded the door so hard it sounded like a sonic boom. "*Are you in there?*"

"Yes," she called back. "I told you I could fit."

Swearing, and then, "Come out of there right now—that's an order!"

Cameryn ignored this. "I was going to unlock the door but there's just a keyhole on this side," she cried, loud enough for him to hear. "I don't get it."

"That's because Leather Ed was paranoid. He used

double key deadbolts to make sure nobody could break into his house. You have to have the key to get out."

"So where is it?"

A pause, and then, "Where's *what*?"

"The key."

"I—he—Leather Ed kept them on his self." Smacking the door again, he cried, "Okay, you've proved your point, you're a very resourceful and independent girl—"

"Woman," Cameryn said. She bit the edge of her lip.

"*Woman*. Now come out of there."

"No."

She said it so softly she knew he couldn't hear her through the door. Doing something on her own was critical in a way she couldn't define. The protective bubble-wrap needed to be ripped away. As she formed a plan in her mind, Cameryn felt more like herself than she had in weeks. It seemed as though she were finally shaking off the fog of sleep. Her mind was humming again.

The sheriff pounded wood, his thumps coming as rapidly as blows from a jackhammer. "Get yourself back through that doggy door right now!"

Cameryn stood close to the door, her palm resting on the cool wood. "Listen, I'm going to find Leather Ed and get the keys. Then I'll open the door. It's the most logical thing to do. So just chill."

"Cameryn Mahoney!" Jacobs roared, and Cameryn knew enough to jump back. The sheriff reached his arm through the dog door shoulder deep, cursing in frustration as his hand grabbed nothing but air. There was no way he could fit through the opening. He knew it, too.

Cameryn tuned out the pounding, concentrating instead on what she might find in the next room. Though the dim half-light she moved forward, the smell thickening with every step. Cupping her hand over her nose, Cameryn walked into a room filled with trash, with only a tiny rabbit trail, a foot wide, winding between mounds of newspapers and old magazines.

So, Leather Ed, this is your living room. A recliner had been shoved against a battered sofa covered with an afghan. Both were empty. The television had been left on but there was no sound. The weatherman pointed to different points on a map, his mouth moving silently as the light blinked against the walls.

Strange, she thought as she took in the disarray. *What a weird, sad man.* She remembered waiting on Leather Ed at the Grand right before Christmas, when she and the cook had surreptitiously watched him muttering to himself. Cameryn had noticed the way the cowhide conformed to his body until it became a kind of shell. The smell of unwashed flesh engulfed him, and his gray hair sprang from his head in a kind of tangled wire. Like everyone else her age, she'd steered clear of the man. Now, inhaling the distinctive odor that told her Leather Ed was most surely dead, she felt ashamed of herself. *Maybe the town overwhelmed you, just like it's overwhelming me*, she thought. *Were you trying to escape us?* But even as she thought it she knew it wasn't true. He'd walked among them, but he'd been invisible. The town was trying to escape *him*.

She moved on.

The smell was more intense by the staircase. Blinking, she looked up into the dark that stretched above her. The stair creaked beneath her foot when she took a tentative step, her hand gliding on the wooden railing as she began her ascent.

Sheriff Jacobs's cries were muted now and easier to ignore. From this distance the sheriff's rapping sounded like a pencil tapping against a desk as she stepped into the upper hallway. And then there was another sound, a voice that made her chest tighten. It was louder than Sheriff Jacobs's. More urgent. Angrier.

"Cammie, it's me, Justin. You've got to stop this *right now*! It's not safe!"

She groaned. As protective as her father and Sheriff Jacobs had been, Justin, Silverton's deputy, had been worse. Still, she was committed to her path. Let them yell. All would be forgiven when she got those keys.

A door was on her right, cracked open less than an inch. Cautious, she pushed against it. Hinges squeaked loudly as the door swung open and she registered a stench strong enough to taste. Pulling her shirt over her nose, she breathed through the cotton, grateful for this barest protection.

It took a moment for her eyes to adjust. Shadows seemed to float against the wall like underwater creatures. Through the murky light she strained to see. Her fingers found the switch plate and she flipped it on. And there, propped in a chair by the bed, was the bloated corpse of Leather Ed, a book clutched in his hands. Body fluid had seeped onto the pages, covering the lines of print in an eerie watercolor. His feet, still encased in worn boots, were planted on the floor while his leathers, distended from decomposition, shone in the light. But it was his face that made Cameryn's mind freeze. Every bit of flesh was gone from his eyes down to his neck. His teeth, white and gleaming, grinned at her from a stripped skull. His jawbone had been wiped clean.

She could feel the horrified expression on her face as the room began to wobble at the edges of her periphery. Forcing her breathing to slow, Cameryn tried to make herself think rationally.

The German shepherd must have gotten to the corpse. His dog did this. From her forensic studies she knew animals could consume their masters after death. *You've still got to get the keys. Keep going,* she commanded as she moved closer to the body.

She wouldn't have noticed the piece of paper folded neatly on the end table next to the body but for her name. The word *Cameryn* had been printed with beautiful precision.

She reached out and grabbed the parchment, written in a perfect cursive hand.

To Cameryn, my anam cara,

I will love you until your dying breath. Please believe that I will find you, my Angel of Death. We are bound by cords you cannot break. Two worlds, intersecting separate pieces that the fates will never break apart. Trust that I will be with you soon.

In eternal adoration,
Kyle O'Neil

Chapter Two

BY THE TIME she made it back to the kitchen door Cameryn felt her composure begin to crack. *Thud thud thud*—the sound of her own heartbeat drummed in her ears as she tried to get the key into the keyhole but her hands were shaking too hard. The tip of the key slipped to the side, leaving a scratch on the brass, until on the third try the deadbolt gave way. Before the sheriff could say a word she thrust the note into his hands.

"Leather Ed is dead," she gasped. Although she'd been running, her skin had grown unbelievably cold. Her heart pounded against her sternum like a fist. She tried not to meet Justin's gaze as he stared at her with a look of horror but instead spoke directly to the sheriff.

"This was left next to Leather Ed. Kyle—he's been

here. I don't know how long ago he left, but he was *in* that house."

"What the . . . ?" Jacobs's face twisted as his eyes skimmed the note's precise handwriting. Justin, who had finished reading first, began to pace across the back end of the porch, the soles of his boots striking wood in beats that matched the thumping of her heart. The sheriff read it a second time before looking at her with narrowed eyes. "You think Kyle could still be inside?"

Cameryn shook her head. "No. I was pretty much through the place. I think I would have seen him."

"Oh, man," Justin cried softly. "You should never have gone in there by yourself."

"From the decomp I'd say Leather Ed's been dead at least two weeks. He—his face is gone. I think it was the dog. . . ."

"What you think is irrelevant, Cammie. We're gonna need help." The sheriff snapped open his phone to place an emergency call to the Durango police, requesting backup, while Justin began to pace again. Cameryn stood in a pool of isolation as Jacobs barked orders into the phone. Concentrating hard, she tried to keep her emotional numbness from thawing. Because she didn't want to feel. If she let in the horror of what had happened she would fall apart, and that was the last thing she wanted to do. Yet, against her will, her thoughts jumped back to the night Kyle had tried to kill her. In her mind's eye she could see Kyle's dark shape looming on the snow as he'd watched her while she, frozen, stared back. *Are you afraid, Cammie? I have a sixth sense. It's strange—I can almost smell it when people are full of fear.* Kyle would be happy to know that she was terrified.

Across the street a motion caught her eye. It was from a curtain, pulled open less than an inch in a dark slash. Was *he* watching her from that window? Then the curtain flicked shut, the movement almost imperceptible, and suddenly she felt eyes everywhere. They were in the houses that lined the street. Eyes stared at her from behind trees, peering from the evergreen bushes that formed natural huts along walkways. The full weight of what she'd done came crashing down. She'd gone into a house where Kyle had been and she had stood where he had stood. The thought made her head whirl.

"You're one lucky girl." The skin on Jacobs's face had paled to a paper white but when he spoke his voice remained all business. "Go home, Cameryn," he commanded. Justin, who had stopped by the sheriff's side, nodded curtly.

Confused, she asked, "Wait—don't you want me to show you where the body is?"

This time it was Justin who spoke. "You can't be a

part of this. You're part of the case now." Justin, the deputy she'd always been drawn to, stood unyielding in his almost-uniform—his jeans topped by a heavy regulation parka, a badge hanging on a cord around his neck. Dark, too-long hair hung into a thick fringe of lashes, obscuring eyes that were blue or green, depending on his mood.

"My deputy is right." The sheriff squatted and grabbed her parka. "It's a conflict of interest."

"But—"

"You do bodies, Cameryn, not investigations. You've screwed this one up already." With his right hand he held up the note, his eyes narrowing into slits. "This should have been left exactly where you found it and dusted for prints. You took the keys from Leather Ed's pocket, another error. I can't afford mistakes. And it's a good thing you've been traumatized by this psycho or I would have traumatized your ass myself for not listening to me in the first place. Here." Jacobs tossed Cameryn her parka. "Put this on and adios. That's an order."

It was useless to fight them. She yanked on her parka, now cold from being left on the porch. And then she felt his warmth at her side. An arm embraced her, pulling her close. Justin.

"I don't think Cameryn should be alone," Justin said, his voice floating above her head. "It's not safe."

Jacobs nodded. Every muscle in his body seemed locked into place. "I was thinkin' the same thing. Take her home in the squad car. Leave the wagon here so we can load the remains. Patrick—your father"—he shot Cameryn another piercing look—"ought to be here any minute, and I think it would be best if you hightailed it out of here before he shows up."

Justin's blue-green eyes met the sheriff's gray ones. There seemed to be a silent conversation between the two of them as Justin's arm tightened around Cameryn's shoulders so hard she almost winced. Looking up, she saw the silver scar on his chin, fine as a strand of hair glinting in winter sun.

"Watch her, Deputy. Anything"—Jacobs emphasized the word—"*anything* can happen now."

Once again Cameryn felt as though she'd become a child. Back beneath the suffocating mantle of protection, yet grateful for the security, she allowed herself to be led to the patrol car. Stoic, Justin opened the passenger door and reminded her to put on her seat belt. The car roared to life as he pushed hard on the gas pedal, but she didn't have the energy to chide him about speeding. Outside, the houses of Silverton, old Victorians painted in candy colors, whizzed by. The homes were as different as the people who owned them. One porch was filled with abandoned items: an old couch with bedding draped over the railing, while the next house, painted a soft yellow, sported a walk-way shoveled so precisely the path looked geometric. Two extremes living side by side, just like the emotions that raged in her. Security and independence. Fear and safety. What was she supposed to do with the contradictions? She was now, more than ever, pulled back into the undertow of Kyle O'Neil.

They were barely on Greene Street when Justin uttered one word: "Why?"

She looked at him blankly. "Why what?"

"Why did you do it? I've told you over and over again to be careful and you went in there *alone*." He choked on the last word.

Cameryn closed her eyes. "Please, Justin, don't start. This has already been a really bad day." She almost laughed at how ridiculously small the word sounded. Bad. Three letters that should have been three thousand. But because they were friends, she forced herself to come up with an explanation. "I guess—I thought I could help."

"Help?" There was genuine anger in Justin's voice, a new sharpness she'd never heard directed at her before. "You're seventeen—a teenager—so what is it? You think bad things can't happen to you? That you're unbreakable?" He snapped his head in her direction. "I've got news for you, Cameryn. It doesn't work that way."

She stiffened in her seat, more hurt than angry. "I know I'm a mortal. I get it. But I'm not a child."

"Then stop acting like one!"

Now it was Cameryn's turn to feel the heat in her cheeks. Glaring at him, she asked, "Why are you doing this? I don't want to talk right now, okay? Just take me home. My mammaw and my dad'll ground me until summer, if that makes you feel any better, but right now I'm asking you to leave it alone."

"You don't get it, do you?"

"Just . . . stop." Too many emotions crowded inside for her to make room for another lecture. She was too strung out for a fight, especially with Justin. In the past he'd always been the one to steady her and yet now he was making things worse. "I just want to forget about today," she pleaded.

"Right. Typical Cameryn Mahoney response. You shut things down when it gets hard. But not this time. Not when the stakes are this high." When he looked at her the pain in his eyes was unconcealed. "Don't you understand that I worry about you? All the time. Every minute of every day."

Cameryn swallowed, her throat suddenly so dry she wasn't sure if she could make a sound come out. She felt a tilt inside that she tried to dismiss, because what she sensed might be happening was something she could not deal with any more than she could comprehend the meaning of Kyle's *I'll love you until your dying breath*. Shrugging, in what she hoped looked like nonchalance, she whispered, "I can take care of myself."

"That's just the point—you can't as long as *he's* out there! Don't you know I drive by your house every night, watching, trying to make sure you're safe? All my free time's gone to tracking this guy." His voice broke, a sound like ice cracking. "You're so young."

"What does my age have to do with any of this?"

"Nothing. Everything." Justin hit the steering wheel with the palm of his hand. "Cameryn, I'm so crazy right now I can't even think straight. Can you imagine what that monster would do to you if he got the chance? With that device of his? It could have been a trap. He could have used that thing on you."

Cameryn winced at the picture of Kyle and his klystron, a death machine of his own design. Microwaved flesh and a locker full of bones, stacked up like children's blocks. These were the images she would never forget. She pressed her forehead into the cool glass, closing her eyes, trying to erase the images that burned behind her eyelids.

"If anything ever happened to you . . ." He couldn't finish the thought.

She could see his reflection in the car's windshield, a faint echo of the man who was driving too fast down Greene Street toward the mountains. Six months ago, when he'd left New York to become Silverton's new deputy, Justin had burst into her world like a comet. But he was twenty-one to her seventeen, and in the end she'd walked away, mostly because he could pierce her soul in a way no one else could. Now there was a fierceness in him that belied the label they'd both accepted: friends. Hadn't he agreed to that definition? And yet his face at that moment seemed anything but friendly. This wasn't about just about Kyle.

He turned west and followed the narrow switchback road in silence before he saw what he wanted. With a whiplike motion he swerved into a pullout, an arc of dirt cut into a crescent. The earth seemed to drop away into a sheer valley thick with pine. The car shuddered as he cut the engine and Cameryn realized how very quiet it was beneath the granite walls.

The silence felt awkward. There was a charge in the atmosphere, neutrons bumping protons, making heat. To break the tension she touched his arm. "Look, I'm sorry I freaked you out but I'm okay. I promise. Quit worrying about me."

"That's not going to happen."

In this close space she could smell him, the intoxicating fragrance of leather mixed with the scent of his skin. She was aware of his breathing, the in, the out. It was late, almost five o'clock, and the sky had darkened to a mountain twilight. A car drove by, throwing light, and she could see him more clearly for a moment, the dark halo of hair and his brows knotting together. The air they exhaled clouded the glass until the windshield turned the color of milk.

"Justin, what are we doing here?"

"We're here because there are . . . things to say."

"Then say them. If I don't get home soon my mammaw will call the FBI."

His face looked pained. "You make it sound easy."

"But you've always been able to talk to me."

He gripped the steering wheel so hard his knuckles jutted in small peaks. "You know, I'm not afraid to hunt down Kyle, but I'm actually scared to put this on the table. Bullets are easier. Easier than these words, anyway." Ducking his head, he paused, and as the silence swelled, her nervousness did, too. Instinctively she knew to keep very still, like a rabbit in tall grass. Her breathing became shallow as she waited. Justin cleared his throat.

"Cammie, you know—you *have* to know—that I care about you."

"I care about you, too," she said reflexively. "Like you said, we're friends, right?"

"Yes. No, I . . . it's more complicated than that. Cammie, I care about you more than I should. More than friends. Enough to land me in prison, since you're underage." Justin smiled his familiar crooked grin, but it was the look in his eyes that made her panic.

No, not now. Not now. The conversation she'd both

wanted and feared was actually happening and she couldn't unlock her mind. It was too much and her thoughts refused to line up. Less than an hour ago she had stood over a body and read a note threatening her life. And yet here was a chance to walk away from that darkness straight into air and sunlight. *Why not?* she asked herself while another, louder voice told her she was crazy to even think of tangling up her life.

Suddenly his hand was on hers, rough and warm. "When I realized how close you came to getting hurt, I had a certain . . . clarity. I know what I want, Cammie. I don't want to wait any more."

As she looked down her hair fell into her lap in dark tendrils. Hiding behind that dark wall, she whispered, "Justin." She wasn't sure what she was about to say until the words came from her mouth. "This isn't the right time."

His fingers were in her hair, gently twisting strands. "That's just the point. It's never the right time. When I tried to ask you the first time, you chose Kyle instead of me. I thought, good—it's a sign, it means she's too young. Then after Kyle left I decided to try my luck again."

She barely said the words. "You did?"

He nodded. "Except that's when your mother showed up in Silverton and I decided . . . I told myself, stop—Cameryn can't take more pressure. But Hannah's gone back to New York, and you're here." He moved closer, his eyes fixed on hers, as green as pine reflecting in mountain water. "I'm here," he whispered. "And Kyle's *out there*. I just want to keep you safe."

She couldn't think anymore because she didn't want to. He touched her cheek, his fingertip rough against her skin. Tracing the curve of her chin, Justin leaned close until his forehead lingered less than an inch from hers. It was the first time he'd ever touched her like that, like a man to a woman, and she closed her eyes, shivering at the possibilities. Almost ready to let herself go, she felt just as she had with Kyle, but *that* letting go had gone horribly wrong and she was too scared to try again. She pulled away, hating herself when she saw the look in Justin's eyes.

"What?" He sounded confused. "Are you saying no?"

"I'm . . . I . . ." She shook her head. "I don't know what I'm saying. No, that's not exactly true. I'm saying . . . wait. Please. Until I can figure this out. Justin, there's no way I can do anything more right now than survive. I've got to deal with the fact that Kyle's trying to kill me. Can you understand that?"

"Do I have a choice?" It was quiet for a moment. He dropped his head against the headrest and let out a long sigh.

"I'm sorry," she said in a small voice.

"No, Cammie, I'm the one who is sorry. I made a mistake. Announcing my intentions right now was not the best move." More silence filled the air until it ballooned into every crevice. Headlights from another vehicle slid along the road before they disappeared around a bend, and as Cameryn watched those lights she wished she could vanish, too. Justin's quiet breathing intertwined with her own shallow breaths until finally, when she couldn't take it anymore, she said, "It's just—this day has been . . . surreal." It surprised her when she realized tears had welled in her eyes. Something inside her had cracked and she could feel her control slipping. She was not a crier, never a crier. She tried to look up at the ceiling of the car so they wouldn't spill over but she felt Justin's hand on her cheek. He was suddenly only inches away. Gently, he wiped the hot tears with the pad of his thumb. "Cammie, it's okay."

"No, it's not. Whatever this is, Justin, it's *not* okay. I make a mess out of everything. I mean—just look at what I did to the case—Sheriff Jacobs hates me now. If Kyle doesn't murder me my dad will, and now *you're* upset with me and—"

"I'm not upset."

Cameryn paused, aware of how close Justin's face was to hers. Her mind reeled as she whispered, "You're not?"

"No. We're still friends, right?"

"Yes. Of course."

"And when Kyle is taken care of we can move on." It was a statement, not a question.

"Justin, I *want* to, but—"

"But my timing sucks," he broke in. Softly, he added, "The thing is, you've just upped my motivation to get Kyle O'Neil." His lips were close, too close. She could smell cinnamon on his breath and the clean scent of his skin as her thoughts spun like a whirligig.

"Justin . . ." She couldn't finish because she no longer knew what she wanted to say.

He pulled away and placed his hands on the steering wheel. "I'd better get you home."

The engine roared as he backed up, the end of the car spinning against ice. "One thing you should know," he said, shifting as he accelerated onto the Million Dollar Highway, "when I say 'get' Kyle, I don't just mean catch him. I'm going to find him and make sure he never hurts anyone again."

Chapter Three

"SO JUSTIN'S REALLY into you, just like I told you he was from the very beginning," Lyric proclaimed in the school lunchroom, her kohl-rimmed eyes opened so wide Cameryn could see the whites all around. "I *said* he liked you, remember? Now the romance is *finally* about to happen! And I can't believe the man checks out your house at night—the way Justin's trying to protect you is *hot*." Lyric, her best friend since grade school, pumped her chubby fist in the air and made a whooping sound so loud everyone in the cafeteria turned to stare. At least, to Cameryn, it felt that way.

"Lyric," Cameryn begged. "Stop."

"Why should I? This is good stuff. And you, ever-cautious one, should go for it. Besides, I would think this Kyle thing would really up your *'carpe diem'* factor. Come on, Cammie, seize the day!"

Over the clanking plastic trays and hum of lunch-time conversation, Cameryn heard another, more sinister sound: the current of gossip, a riptide of innuendo that she was forced to wade through once again. Cameryn saw it in the way heads bent together, the concerned looks being shot her way, the thrilled sympathy that made her want to crawl away and hide. Only Lyric seemed oblivious to the drama being played out all around. Leaning forward, she put her hand on Cameryn's arm and said, "Listen, it's going to work out between the two of you. I'm a psychic—I know."

"Why don't you tune your psychic powers to another channel?" Cameryn hissed. "People are staring."

"Not a chance. I'm digging this one." Lyric shook her hair, this time dyed black and cut with swaths of ruby red. In many ways Cameryn's opposite, Lyric was the closest thing to a sister Cameryn had ever had. And yet, from the outside, everything about the two of them seemed paradoxical. Lyric towered over Cameryn, both in height and personality. While Cameryn's wardrobe consisted mainly of hoodies and jeans, Lyric favored loud colors that reflected her mood. Today she wore a peasant blouse tie-dyed in every shade of orange, black jeans, and platform shoes that made her taller than most of their teachers. Every finger on her hand sported a chunky ring, each a different jewel color that bumped against the others like a plastic rainbow. Honey brows revealed her natural shade of hair, while her pale blue eyes seemed to brighten and darken with her moods. In contrast, Cameryn felt she was a plain brown package. Dark hair, brown eyes, simple jeans, no flash. It was lucky that Lyric had enough character for the two of them.

"So when do you think you'll move up from the air kiss to the real deal? My spider sense is tingling."

"See, this is exactly why I should never tell you anything. I think Tiffany just heard you."

"Sorry," Lyric replied in an exaggerated whisper. "But since when did you start caring about *them*? We've been rebels since fifth grade, remember?" She waved her hand dismissively toward the corner table. "And who worries about what Tiffany and her Bratz posse thinks? Actually, that might be an oxymoron." Tapping her chin thoughtfully, she added, "I don't believe Tiffany actually thinks. "

"Great. Now she's whispering to Heather."

Lyric frowned. "You know what your problem is, Cameryn Mahoney?"

"Having a friend who seeks divine guidance from transparent minerals?"

"You're hilarious today. No, it's the fact that you're too much into facts. You need to expand your mind beyond the constraints of science. So, to get back to the point, I've always known how you felt about Justin even when you were in deep denial. Quit throwing up roadblocks and go after the guy. You might as well do it because I see it in your future anyway."

Cameryn snorted. It was an old argument between them, one that would never be resolved. Like two puppies tugging on a rope, they chewed on philosophy and religion from different ends in a never-ending battle. Picking up a carrot stick, she took a bite and wagged it in Lyric's face. "See, this is why I question your psychic powers—the 'information'"— Cameryn made quotes in the air with her fingers—"provided by your 'feelings' is never actually useful. I don't need your 'inner eye' blinking over Justin. It's Kyle I'm worried about. Tell me where he is, and I'll buy some tarot cards."

"It doesn't work that way and you know it." Lyric rolled her eyes. "God, you're such a skeptic."

"And this would be the part where you refuse to admit you are wrong—"

A voice, smoky yet smooth, cut into their conversation. "Ladies, ladies, this isn't a time to fight." The voice belonged to Adam, Lyric's boyfriend. Long and sharp boned, Adam looked even more angular next to Lyric's curvy figure as he slid onto the bench beside her. He wore, as always, his usual black, although today his tee shirt sported a pirate's skull with an eye patch that glowed in the dark. Adam's fish-white skin looked even paler next to his hair, which, dyed the color of ink, hung in sheets to his shoulders. His fingernails, tipping long fingers, had been painted a metallic green. He put a thin arm around Lyric as he shot a look at Cameryn. "Now is the time for peace."

"Exactly." Lyric nodded, looking smug. Crossing her arms, she leaned into Adam's shoulders, saying, "Okay, so check this out. Justin has finally made his move, which I was *trying* to talk about, but Cameryn being Cameryn of course changed the subject and is instead belittling my psychic powers. I think it's her way of avoiding emotional subjects. Cameryn tends to repress instead of express. Not a healthy way to be."

"Lyric," Cameryn said, narrowing her eyes.

"What?"

"Shut up."

Adam looked nervously from one to the other, but Lyric and Cameryn each threw a fry at the other, snickering as they dodged their bad throws. It was hard for an outsider to understand how Cameryn and Lyric worked. Their squabbling was a way to anchor Cameryn to life, because Lyric knew Cameryn almost as well as she knew herself. It had been Lyric who'd shown up in her bedroom that morning. After Kyle's note, Cameryn had thought of staying home, but Lyric had insisted that Cameryn get up and come to school. "Come on, slacker. Rise and shine."

"No," Cameryn had murmured, clutching her pillow over her head. "Mammaw says I don't have to go if I don't want to." This had been a first: her grandmother, called Mammaw after the Irish way, had told Cameryn that under the circumstances she could stay home for the rest of the year if she wanted. But Lyric would hear none of it.

"What are you going to do," Lyric had demanded, "hide underneath your sheets forever? Screw that! If Kyle keeps you afraid, he wins. Besides, nothing's going to happen on *my* watch." Yanking the bed covers onto the floor, Lyric, with her large frame, had loomed over Cameryn, who had curled herself into a protective ball. "Don't forget I'm bigger than he is. At least my curves are good for something. Get *up*! We're going to be late."

Now, sitting in the cafeteria, surrounded by the familiar rhythms of life, Cameryn realized that Lyric had been right. The smell of the rubbery burgers, the safe, institutional walls, all made the fear fade back to a place where she could manage it. Kyle couldn't get her in school, not in this solid building where people milled around her like cattle in a stockyard. No one could.

Adam rubbed his chin with his long fingers, his green polish flashing like scales. "Since talking about you and Justin is more of a girly thing, I would like to switch the subject back to the murder of Leather Ed."

"No one's sure if it was murder," Cameryn corrected.

"They won't know what killed him until the autopsy."

"Ri-ight." He drawled the word. His hands moved up his face until he stopped at his forehead, which he began to tap in a staccato rhythm. "So you got bounced from the case because of the note, which makes sense since you're the subject of said document. That constitutes an obvious conflict of interest."

"Adam's thinking of studying law," Lyric whispered conspiratorially. "You should listen to him."

"And there are, like, six versions of the note floating around. Just out of curiosity, what did Kyle say?" He was trying to sound nonchalant, but Cameryn could sense by the way he leaned in that he was as excited to hear the details as everyone else. She was distracted as Tiffany and her pack of friends breezed by, their whispers trailing like a wake. Cameryn watched them and tried not to listen as her name bobbed softly along their waves. Their muted laughter sounded like water slapping the shoreline. *You know she loves the attention . . . Kyle O'Neil . . . work with the dead, that's what you get . . . freak.*

"Come on, Cammie," Adam pressed, "the hallways are buzzing with the news. This is big-time stuff—local girl gets stalked by deranged killer who leaves a love note etched in blood."

"It wasn't in blood, it was ink," Cameryn said woodenly. She picked up a French fry and pushed a mound of catsup to one side of her tray, trying to make her face look as though she hadn't heard a word of the hushed conversation. But Lyric was way ahead of her.

"Ignore them," she said fiercely. Lyric's eyes burned as she hissed, "They are idiots."

Adam looked up in surprise. His gaze bounced from Lyric to Cameryn to Lyric again. "Ignore who? Wait a minute, what am I missing here?"

"Being a typical guy," Lyric replied, "that would be everything." She swelled in her orange peasant top, her red hair catching the light like flames. "Don't let them get to you."

The other girls in her school—most of the students, Cameryn guessed—had always seen her as an outsider. She'd first been tainted by her high academic marks and then shunned for her love of forensics. When she'd become assistant to the coroner they began to call her the Angel of Death, cutting a swath around her in the hallways as if her passion was contagious. It was Kyle who had changed her spot in the teen hierarchy. For a blazing moment she'd ridden his coattails to popularity until she was finally acknowledged by Tiffany and company. Cameryn had almost believed the girls with the empty eyes would see her as more than a science geek. But after Kyle disappeared, their attention had, too. It was, as always, Lyric, Adam, and now Justin who stood by her. She would never again forget who her real friends were.

"The note?" Adam prodded.

Winter light poured through the cafeteria's high windows, and through the glass Cameryn could see the flash of an airplane's wing. The school's yellow brick walls gave off sunny warmth as Cameryn retold the story. Resting his chin on his palm, Adam seemed mesmerized until the last syllable. "Wow," he breathed. "How did your dad take all this?"

"Exactly the way you'd expect. Now he tells me I can't go anywhere except to school and to work. He needs to know where I am at every single exact second. Mammaw's at the church lighting enough candles to burn the place down." Attempting a smile, she added, "On the upside, Dad's finally cool with Justin. I guess he likes the idea of me hanging out with a man who wears a gun. But, as I was just saying to Lyric"—she shot her friend a look—"I don't know if I'm ready just yet."

"Wow," Adam said again. "You're talking about going out with Justin, like, officially?"

"Well, yeah, that's the general idea."

"But you're only seventeen. Isn't that illegal?" His eyebrows arched up into his pale, narrow forehead. "Not that there's anything wrong with that."

Cameryn gave an exaggerated shrug. "It's not illegal, and anyway I'll be eighteen soon. And I'm not even sure yet what I'm going to do. I've got Kyle to deal with."

"Besides, even if it *was* illegal," Lyric added, "what would Justin do? Arrest himself?"

Adam snickered as he buried his face in Lyric's dyed hair.

"All right, you two, enough!" Cameryn cried. "This conversation is over."

Lyric rubbed her hands together with glee. "No, I see it. I feel Justin's vibe and it's strong. He's thinking of you right now!"

As if on cue, Cameryn's BlackBerry hummed in the pocket of her jeans. Her eyes widened as she realized it was Justin, calling during school. *Odd*, she thought. Tossing her hair back, she pressed her phone to her ear. "Hey, what's going on?" *Justin,* she mouthed to Lyric, who responded with a thumbs-up.

"Cammie, I need to know what the rest of your day looks like," Justin said. His words were quick, sharp. "As in your schoolwork, I mean. Your pop says it's okay as long as your schoolwork is cool. Is it?"

"Yeah, I'm good. But what—"

Justin cut her off. "It's Dr. Moore. He wants you in the autopsy suite right now."

It took Cameryn a moment to register the information. The bell rang, signaling the end of lunch, and she could barely think above the screeching of the metal legs against ancient linoleum as the room disgorged itself of students. Trays clattered one on top of another, bodies bumped in a line as leftovers were dumped through the revolving plastic lid.

"Wait, Justin, if this is about Leather Ed, I'm not allowed to work the case."

"It's not Leather Ed. This is . . . something else."

Lyric leaned close, the fabric of her peasant shirt drooping like orange wings. "I told you I felt his vibe," she whispered into Cameryn's free ear. "Who's got the power?"

Shaking her head, Cameryn frowned and held up her index finger. "So who died?" she asked.

"I'm not sure. All I can tell you is that this whole thing is freakin' weird. Dr. Moore says the inside of the first body is not like anything he's ever seen before. He wants to wait to begin the second autopsy until you're there."

Cameryn blinked. "Excuse me—did you say *second* autopsy?"

Students shuffled past, their feet digging forward as they chewed on the last of their lunches, hurrying toward the exit. Cameryn's whole mind focused on the word *second*. *Two* deaths. Two bodies, prepped to be dissected and reassembled like pieces of a puzzle.

Justin paused and added, "This is the first time I've heard Moore ask for help."

That fact alone seemed impossible. Dr. Moore, the curmudgeon pathologist from Durango, stomped through his autopsy suite like an aging bull, barking orders at everyone within earshot. And yet he wanted Cameryn's presence. She could feel her internal gears shifting as she flipped into her scientific mode. "Do you know the manner of death?"

"No idea. These guys keeled over and dropped dead in some restaurant. Boom—they were gone. Moore told me to tell you that this case is 'sensitive.' That translates to: keep it under the radar for now."

Lyric pulled at the edge of Cameryn's sleeve. "Cammie, what's going on?" she asked, at the same time as Justin fired his next question.

"So, are you in?"

"Of course I'm in." Then, to Lyric, she whispered, "It's forensic stuff. I've got to go."

"I'm sorry, Cammie," Justin apologized. "I was hoping to keep you away from the stressful stuff and this is definitely not what I had in mind."

"No worries." She tried to ignore the way her stomach wobbled when she thought about spending time alone with Justin. It was better this way, having a focus. It made her less nervous.

The last of the departing students whirled past like confetti, blurring in the edge of her periphery. "I'll go to the front office and check myself out. Where are you now?" Cameryn asked. She slid out of her chair and onto her feet, stacking her tray neatly on top of Lyric's.

"I'm out in front. Hurry, Cameryn. I'm already waiting."

Chapter Four

"YOU READY FOR this?" Justin asked.

"Yeah. Are you?" Cameryn replied. The two of them climbed the cement steps of the Durango Medical Examiner's Building. She'd never entered by the front before. Instead she and her father, in their station wagon hearse, had always arrived via the garage. Now as she and Justin stood side by side she studied their reflection shimmering in the glass door. With a start she realized how much he towered over her—a good eleven inches separated the top of her head from his.

I look so young, she thought. Her dark hair, which hung past her mid back, made her look every bit the teenager she was. The blue Land's End parka and faded jeans didn't help. Instinctively she rocked slightly onto her toes, adding a modicum of height, which made her feel better somehow.

"Just how short are you, anyway?"

He must have seen her stretching. "Tall enough to cut up a body," she replied.

"Point taken." Smiling, he pushed open the door and ushered her inside. That was how it had been the entire drive down—they'd kept it light, talking about the case and the urgency of Dr. Moore's call. They both knew they had sailed into new waters, and yet Justin, thankfully, was giving her space. Still, there was an unspoken tide moving just beneath the surface. She could feel it in the way his gaze lingered on hers a beat longer than before, the way he let his hand graze against hers, his fingers light against her skin. He was holding back, waiting, watching for her "yes."

"You know, no matter how hard they scrub it, this place still reeks of death," Justin whispered into the top of her head. "I'd rather smell your hair."

"You mean my dandruff shampoo."

"Ah, is that what it is?" He took in a deep whiff. "Nice."

"You like the smell of salicylic acid and selenium sulfide?"

"You're showing off, Cammie."

"Well, you *did* call me short."

"A mistake I will never make again," he said. "You know too many big words."

"Right. Okay, Justin, you need to be serious. Two people are dead and we're on duty. Focus."

"You want me to be serious?" Thrusting out his chin, he said, "I wish it was Kyle on that autopsy table. He's the one who should be dead. But the universe isn't always fair, is it?"

"You worry too much about me," she answered. Without thinking she laced her fingers through his, and she noticed the corner of his mouth bend up as he squeezed her hand, then released it. Without a word they walked on.

The foyer had a ficus tree propped in a corner; the tips of its branches brushed her as she walked past. Justin was right—there was a smell, a faint sickly sweet odor masked by disinfectant. Noisome traces of the dead. If she believed what Lyric told her, the human cells floating through the building were already being pulled into the soil to be reborn through the leaves in an endless cycle of rebirth in an endless succession.

Cameryn, though, had been raised on the certainty of science intertwined with the mystery of her Catholic faith. It was through these diverse filters that she attempted to explain the uncertainty of justice. How was it that two people had died while Kyle roamed free? She had to believe Kyle would be caught because of forensics, and if science didn't nail him she'd settle for the hand of God, Old Testament style.

After making their way down the hallway they

stopped at a desk made of blond wood. A woman Cameryn vaguely recognized looked up.

"Hey, Justin. Who's your little friend?" She eyed Cameryn's pink Swatch watch and her chewed fingernails. Cameryn quickly shoved her hands in her coat pockets.

"This is Cameryn Mahoney," he answered. "Patrick Mahoney's daughter. She's assistant to the coroner. Dr. Moore asked her to come."

"Oh, right." There was the barest of nods. "I remember now. The child prodigy." The woman wore a name tag that read *Amber Murphy*. She was about twenty-five, with short red hair and a heart-shaped face. Her eyes slid back to Justin and she gave him a bright smile. Cameryn noticed Amber had dimples.

"So, Justin, where have you been hiding?" Amber asked. "I haven't seen you in a while."

"I've been on duty, protecting the good people of Silverton."

"We could use a little of that down here in Durango, cowboy. There's a lot of wild things going on in our big city."

"Did you just call Durango a big city?" Justin asked, laughing. "Remember, I moved here from New York—"

"Excuse me, can we go back now?" Cameryn interrupted. "Dr. Moore made it sound like the case is time sensitive."

Amber blinked, as though she had already forgotten Cameryn was there. Clearing her throat, she said, "Of course. But I'm supposed to ask you a question. Dr. Moore's having a holy fit about security, so . . . did anyone approach you about the decedents at any time before you got here?"

Justin said, "No," while Cameryn shook her head.

"Good. I feel stupid asking, like I'm one of those security people at the airport. I mean, who doesn't know by now *not* to take packages from a stranger, and who'd be dumb enough to say yes if they actually did? But Moore told me to grill everyone, so that's what I'm doing." She leaned forward, and Cameryn noticed that Amber lined her mouth outside the edges. A glossy lipstick glittered on lips painted the color of maple sugar. "Do you even *know* who we got back there?" Amber gave Justin a cloying look. She was talking to him directly while simultaneously erasing Cameryn.

"Not a clue," Justin replied.

But Amber was all smiles. "You'll see." Another knowing look, this time accompanied by a wink as she waved them toward the swinging doors. "One thing's for sure, when this gets out, the paparazzi are gonna go wild," she called after them.

The last words cut in and out as the door swung behind them and Cameryn stopped just beyond their reach. Crossing her arms, she stared up at Justin and hissed, *"Little friend?"*

Justin gave a wicked, faunlike grin, his eyebrows arching into his too-long hair. "Amber's all right."

"I'm sure *you* think so, *cowboy*."

He cocked his head and she felt her heart kick sideways. *Get a grip,* she told herself. She was about to do an autopsy and she had no business musing over the color of Justin's irises, water mixed with sky.

"Is something wrong?" he asked.

"No! It's just that Amber mentioned the word *paparazzi*. Cases that have a lot of media attention are always harder," she lied, aware of how much she disliked Amber and her glossy lips. "Plus, I don't know of any celebrities who live in Durango."

"There's some festival going on in Telluride—I think it's the TelluVision Showcase, or something like that. Telluride's only a couple of hours away. But . . . aren't you the one who said the case was time sensitive?"

"What?"

"You're loitering." He grinned at her in a way that made heat creep up her face. "You chewed out poor Amber and now you're the one standing in the hallway. I could write you up for that."

"You are *such* a punk." Walking quickly, she charged ahead of him to the autopsy room, but before she could push through he grabbed her hand.

"I could let you off for good behavior," he teased. "All you have to do is—"

But whatever he was about to say was interrupted

by a low rumble coming from inside the autopsy suite. "Miss Mahoney, Deputy Crowley—enough with the happy chatter. Get in here. *Now*!" The voice belonged to Dr. Moore. His tone was even more cantankerous than usual.

"I'll review your case later," Justin whispered as he thrust open the door.

The room was large, as big as five of her classrooms, with gleaming chrome and lights that droned like insects in a swamp. The floor, laid with green and white tile, had been scrubbed so often the shine had dulled. Cameryn knew that at times bodies leaked fluid through their body bags to leave trails across the floor. As always the odor was stronger in here, the last traces of life still discernible beneath the fumes of bleach. Huddled around an autopsy table were Dr. Moore; his assistant, Ben; Sheriff Jacobs; and Cameryn's father, Patrick. They all turned to stare as Cameryn and Justin entered the room.

"Well, I'm glad you two finally made it," her father said. Patrick's eyes seemed to linger on Justin a brief moment before flicking away. It was hard to discern what he was thinking because the mask made his expression inscrutable.

"This case will require your full concentration," said Dr. Moore. The doctor, still bent over the body, wore thick gloves and a heavy plastic apron over pale scrubs. His morgue shoes, a pair of black high-tops with Velcro instead of laces, were shiny with blood. Half-moon reading glasses perched on the bridge of his paper mask, magnifying his eyes so that they seemed owl-like; a ring of white hair haloed his balding head. Lately, Cameryn had seen a difference in him. His bullfrog neck had thinned, while his round, apple-shaped torso had diminished so that it resembled a deflated ball. But the voice sounded as petulant as ever.

"Grab the clipboard next to the histology samples, Deputy. I'm going to need everyone on this."

"Yes, sir," Justin said as he quickly moved toward a set of cupboards located by the walk-in refrigerator.

"And now for you." Dr. Moore lasered in on Cameryn. "The sheriff has brought me up to speed concerning your shenanigans at Leather Ed's. I'm surprised. I pegged you as an intelligent girl."

"Woman," she corrected automatically under her breath. She flushed when she realized the doctor had heard her.

Moore bit off each word. "Not. Yet."

She felt the full heat of the doctor's gaze, and as much as she wanted to cringe away, she knew she could not. Although she had learned to like Dr. Moore she also understood he would steamroll over anyone who let him. Carefully arranging her face so that it conveyed strength, rather than the panic she was actually feeling, she said, "I already told the sheriff I was sorry."

"Water under the bridge," Jacobs answered, clearing his throat. He shifted uncomfortably. "Let's move on. We got other fish to fry."

"Yeah, give Cammie a break," Ben jumped in. A diener, Ben assisted Dr. Moore in the most difficult aspects of the forensic job. Every corpse was gently washed by Ben, its skin stitched with sutures so wide they looked like the teeth of a zipper. Organs were dipped in water before dissection, the contents of bowels washed clean, and yet, somehow immune to death's gruesomeness, Ben kept his jovial warmth. "We can't gang up on her, Dr. Moore," he said, shooting her a grin. "Not when we're askin' for her help."

"Well, I see you've got your fan club ready to defend you, Miss Mahoney." Dr. Moore drew in woolly brows. "But I still have a few things to say."

Everyone in the room seemed to draw a collective breath. Moore, seemingly unaware, carefully set down a scalpel so that it lined up perfectly along the edge of the counter. "Here's my problem: I do not want to unzip a body bag to find the remains of the assistant to the coroner tucked inside. Since I am, in essence, mentoring you, I expect you to show a modicum of intellect. O'Neil is a psychopath with a fixation on you. What you did was foolish in the extreme."

"That's enough, Doctor." Patrick Mahoney peeled the tape back and tugged off his mask. He was tall, with white hair as thick as a pelt and skin seamed by a lifetime in the mountains. Ever since she'd been small, Cameryn had learned how to read him. When upset he seemed to swell with emotion, and by the current size of him Cameryn could tell he didn't like Moore dressing her down. "I appreciate what you're saying, but Cameryn is *my* daughter. Mine, not yours. And we've handled it between us."

Moore's eyes snapped from Patrick to Cameryn. The conversation was unspoken now, just between the two of them. "Are we clear, Miss Mahoney?"

"Yes," she answered softly.

"Good. Now come closer. You see this man?"

Obedient, Cameryn walked toward the hollowed body. She could almost taste the blood, yet there was no smell of decay. Even though her fingers weren't gloved she touched his skin. It was cool. From the softness of the arm she guessed he hadn't been dead long. Once again her mind began to whir as she took in the details of what remained—the puzzle pieces were there, just waiting to be assembled.

"Whatever killed him most likely took his friend there as well." Moore jerked his head toward a second autopsy table. Cameryn glanced at the other body. Wrapped in a sheet, the body was shaped like a man's.

His feet made steeples beneath the thin cotton.

"The two vics died just minutes apart," Moore said, redirecting Cameryn to the body that had been opened. "Look there, Miss Mahoney. Tell me what you see."

As she leaned closer, the daughter-girlfriend part of her personality melted away, and in its place rose a scientific passion that drove her to understand the intricacies of the body splayed open beneath her.

Beginning at his feet, Cameryn studied the corpse. The decedent was a slender white man with muscled arms and a tattoo of a dragon snaking up one calf, its fangs bright yellow with eyes the color of garnets. A cloth had been placed discreetly over his groin. Because his scalp had been pulled free and folded beneath his chin, the features of his face had been rendered blank; his skull had been opened and emptied. Cameryn briefly wondered if this man had been famous in life. If he had been, it no longer mattered. There was nothing left to suggest either fame or ignominy. All humans, she knew, were reduced by death to their parts. She stared into the empty space and saw the white knots of his spine gleaming like pearls.

"Well?"

"I'd like to take a look at the organs."

"Very good," Moore said, looking pleased. "That is where the real question lies. To be specific, I'd like you to examine this man's lungs. Here," he said. From a bloodstained towel Dr. Moore plucked a piece of tissue, sliced opened like the pages of a book. "What do you see?"

Whatever disappointment he'd felt toward her for breaking into Leather Ed's had seemingly vanished. In its place was an eagerness, as though the two of them were playing a game where only they understood the rules. "You see what I see? I found it in every lobe."

Fascinated, Cameryn bent so that she was only inches away. The tissue glistened with a coating of clear gel that shimmered like ice. Dr. Moore scraped the viscous matter and rubbed it between his gloved fingers.

"Is this a dry drowning?" she asked.

Again, the smile. "You're on the right track, Miss Mahoney, but no. Dry drowning is caused by the body's delayed reaction to inhaling too much water. But this"—he rubbed his fingers together again—"is not mucus. What you are looking at is a foreign material of unknown origin. The man drowned, yes, but whatever *this* is"—he pulled his fingers apart, the gel forming a thin, tenuous thread—"caused him to drown while sitting in a Durango restaurant. I've never seen anything like it and we have only a short window of time to figure this out before the vultures, and by that I mean the media, swoop in."

"The media?" Cameryn echoed.

"Yes. They're going to accuse me of being a hick pathologist out of my league. I want to be prepared with answers before they do."

Cameryn's heart skipped a beat as she once again looked at the dragon tattoo snaking up the decedent's leg. A memory flashed through her, followed by a sick understanding. "Dr. Moore, who is this man?"

"The lung tissue you're examining belongs to Brent Safer." He gave a cursery nod. "Yes, *the* Brent Safer. The other man is Joseph Stein, world-renowned producer. One of the biggest stars of our time just died in our little town. And when that story breaks . . ." Dr. Moore shut his eyes. He paused, but when he opened them, he looked only at Cameryn. "God help us all."

Chapter Five

"YOU'VE GOT TO be kidding," Justin exclaimed, looking awed. "*This* is Brent Safer? The famous Brent Safer? The Brent Safer who starred in *Raw Fever* and *Blaze*?"

"The very one," Moore replied. "Although I believe action pictures of that caliber to be the lowest kind of tripe. That said, I would like to find some answers before this story breaks. Suit up, Miss Mahoney. I'm counting on your keen eye when we open decedent number two. Ben, my nerves are shot. I need some music."

"Anything in particular, Doctor?" Ben asked genially as he moved to the counter where the boom box was kept. Thickly muscled, Ben moved with a lithe grace Cameryn envied, his shoulders stretching his scrubs thin, his dark skin shining like liquid chocolate.

Everyone knew that Moore was particular about his music. But the doctor surprised her by saying, "Make it anything you like, Ben. Diener's choice."

Ben smiled, flashing teeth. "I don't suppose I could push you far enough for some vintage Tupac Shakur?" Even while asking, Ben shook his head. "Yeah, I didn't think so." He ran his finger along the edge of the CD cases lined up on a shelf. "I'd like to try something a little bit lighter than opera. Hmmm." He plucked a square case from a bottom rack. "This one's got a cover with a ship about to sail off the edge of the world. *Falling Star* by some band called . . . The Seers." He flipped the case from the front to the back, narrowing his lids. "Man, how old is this thing? That's some seriously funky hair."

"They're from the seventies," said Moore. "An inspired choice. Now hustle, Miss Mahoney. I'm expecting an onslaught of the media at any moment."

"Right." Cameryn hurried to the metal storage cabinet, pulling out her gear so that she could quickly suit up: pale green doctor's scrubs were folded beneath a plastic apron with long ties made of twill. From the highest shelf she took down her least favorite piece of gear, a disposable cloth cap to tuck her hair in so that it protruded like a bell. From another shelf she plucked a mask and a pair of latex gloves. In the adjoining locker she found her morgue shoes, and next to them a stack of paper booties. Suiting up, she watched Ben put in the CD, and listened to acoustical instruments float around them, light as summer rain.

"Are you ready?" Moore asked.

"Ready," she answered. She could feel excitement in the air as she moved toward the body of Joseph Stein. A partially filled-out chart on a clipboard lay next to him. On the top she saw a pen fastened by a string.

"They must have been here for the television festival," Cameryn said. "But why wasn't Brent Safer recognized? He's famous."

Her father, jotting down items for the personal inventory, paused long enough to say, "Safer had on a wig and sunglasses, which have already been bagged as evidence. I guess the man wanted to be left alone."

"Wow," Cameryn said. "So no one recognized him?"

"Nope," Ben interjected. "We had no idea who he was until I found his ID. That's when we decided to call you-all—Dr. Moore said he wanted the help."

"That's enough, Ben," Moore grumbled.

"I'm just sayin' that if Stein's got that Jell-O stuff in his lungs then things'll really go crazy."

"Do you want me to unwrap Stein?" Cameryn asked Dr. Moore, but the doctor shook his head vigorously. "There is still an open body that needs to be addressed. Remember, Miss Mahoney, we have procedures and protocols." Once again, although the room was filled with people, the doctor addressed his comments only to her. Just her. It was as if an invisible bubble encased

Cameryn, Ben, and Dr. Moore, shutting out everyone else. The others seemed to sense it, too. She watched as Sheriff Jacobs tilted his head and scratched it, shaking it slowly from side to side while he and Justin exchanged glances. Her father, on the other hand, looked pleased, because he understood this was what she'd always wanted. As coroner, Patrick was limited to the collection and identification of bodies—the basic paperwork of death. Cameryn, though, dreamed of becoming a medical examiner like Dr. Moore. It was the medical examiner who opened up the body. Through autopsies, the ME determined the cause and manner of a victim's death, disassembling and reassembling the decedent's pieces until the picture of what happened became clear. And now, surprisingly, Dr. Moore seemed ready to share his secrets with her. Sensing this, Patrick shot her a knowing smile before jotting another item on the clipboard.

"I can help, sir," Justin said. He took a step toward Cameryn but Dr. Moore waved him away.

"I want to teach my protégée, Deputy, so stand down until you are called." The doctor crossed his arms over his once-ample belly. "We never begin a second autopsy without completing the first. Why, Miss Mahoney?"

Cameryn looked from one disemboweled body to the next, wrapped in a cotton sheet as neatly as a gift. "I don't know."

Tapping his forehead with a gloved finger, Moore said, "Think. Part of your job is to examine the evidence and draw conclusions."

Cameryn bit the edge of her lip, straining for the right answer. Why *would* it make any difference? Mentally, she flipped through the pages of her forensic books, searching for an answer. "Well . . . maybe you'd have to be really careful of any kind of cross-contamination. With two bodies opened up at the same time I suppose there would be a chance that fluid from body A could get into body B, which could screw up the results. Especially if it's a homicide."

Dr. Moore's face lit up, his eyes morning bright as he peered at her over his half-moon glasses. "*Precisely*. When there's any kind of a doubt as to the cause or manner of death, we go by the book. A tight ship means a controlled ship. We go one body at a time. Tools are washed, gloves changed before we begin the dance again. *Constant vigilance*, Miss Mahoney. Constant vigilance, every case, every time."

"You sound like Mad-Eye Moody," Cameryn said.

"Excuse me. Are you trying to be funny?" Dr. Moore lowered his chin, staring at her with eyes that had suddenly lost their warmth. Sheriff Jacobs snorted and leaned against a cabinet, whispering something to her father.

"You know, Mad-Eye? The guy from the Harry Potter

books? Never mind." *Stupid, stupid, stupid*, she chided herself. *Dr. Moore's trying to treat you like a professional and you say something like that.* In an effort to redirect the doctor, she said, "Um, why do you have to wash the tools—don't you have more than one set? I mean, that would seem to make more sense, you know, so you wouldn't have to wait in between bodies."

The skin on the top of Dr. Moore's bald head rippled as the doctor raised his shaggy brows. "I've told you on more than one occasion that we who choose to work on the dark side of medicine suffer from ever-tightening budgets. Saws and scissors are expensive." He held up his index finger and punched the air. "I have *one* diener and *one* set of instruments. Between autopsies everything is washed by hand. Time-consuming, yes, but the dead will be dead for a long time. They don't seem to mind the wait."

By now Ben had come to Cameryn's side, his feet moving in perfect rhythm to the music, trying, Cameryn thought, to lighten to mood. "Hey, Doc, for being an oldie, I have to say I'm down with this Seer thing. The music's got a beat."

Dr. Moore acknowledged Ben by making a sound of approval deep in his throat.

"And Cammie, groovin' to music is the best way to get through the never-ending cleaning of the tools. That's the diener's job, and I'll tell you what, I've had to scrub some nasty things in my time. I go through a boatload of bleach. You want me to show her how it's done, Doc?" he asked, bobbing his head. "I'll wash 'em now if you'd like."

But Dr. Moore surprised them both by saying no. "I will sterilize the equipment myself, Ben," he said. "I'd like Miss Mahoney to watch you sew up our movie star. If she wants to go into this profession she should see every aspect of the procedure, from start to gris-ly finish." Spinning on his heel, he nodded to Justin. "Deputy Crowley, you seem anxious to get in the game. Why don't you assist me by gathering up the tools. You'll find gloves in the cabinet directly to your left. You'll want an apron."

"Of course," Justin answered. He'd been standing with his weight on one leg, his left elbow resting against the countertop. Like a jack-in-the-box he sprang into action, taking out an apron and tying it on so fast his action seemed a blur. Cameryn heard the snap of latex as he pulled on a pair of gloves.

"Well, all right then, Cammie," said Ben, "it looks like today we're all doing our jobs every which way." He made a hook with his arm through the air. "Guess it's just you and me and the celebrity."

Dr. Moore took a plastic tub off a shelf and poured blue-green liquid into it. He set it into the deep metal sink and ran hot water on top, making foam. "Have her wash down the decedent," Dr. Moore called over his shoulder. "Use a casket liner to wrap him. And remember, time is of the essence. The media vultures will discover this soon enough and then all hell will break loose."

"You got it—we'll do it quick and clean," said Ben. A row of instruments had been laid out on a blue towel. From the center he plucked a large, curved needle and began to thread it with black thread. "Wait'll you see, Cammie, this part's kind of fun. We're gonna put the man back together."

Fun was the last word that she would use for it, Cameryn decided. Beginning at the head, Ben picked up a skullcap, still shiny with blood, and placed it back onto Brent Safer's already hollowed-out head. "I told you before about the notch—see? I put it on the cap to make sure the bone lines up just right." He clicked the piece of skull into place like a puzzle piece. "Now let's give this man back his face. Watch how it's done."

With strong fingers, Ben reached down and grabbed the scalp, which had been sliced from ear to ear and tucked beneath Brent Safer's chin. Slowly, carefully, Ben unfolded the face and pulled it toward the dome of the skull. Features, still loose, realigned themselves as Ben clasped the back part of the scalp that had been doubled onto the neck until both flaps met in the middle. She stared down at him, filled with a strange kind of awe. There was the handsome face she'd seen magnified on the movie screen, his skin waxy in death. But the dead Brent Safer was less polished than his Hollywood version. His blond hair, which Cameryn realized had been highlighted, had matted to his skull. Up close she could see faint pits from acne scars, and the skin beneath his eyes was slightly wrinkled, like tissue paper smudged with blue. These imperfections must have been erased by Hollywood makeup artists.

"He looks crooked," Cameryn said.

"Maybe a little," Ben agreed. "But the funeral home'll fix him up nice. If they do their job right then no one will ever be able to tell the man's brain is gone." He began to sew the scalp together with a loose suture. "See, a couple stitches on top of the scalp is all we do 'cause the mortician's gonna take it all out anyway. They'll fluff up his hair and you'll never even see where I cut him. Unless it's a bald dude. You can't do as much with a bald dude except try to hide it with a whole lotta makeup and a big pillow. Good thing Brent Safer had so much hair."

"Yeah. Good thing," she said, gently stroking the hair that made a fringe against his neck. It wasn't until she touched him that the weight of who she was standing near washed through her. This was a man she'd seen on the big screen, his overlarge image flickering in syrupy theater light. In a strange way she felt as if she knew him. Lyric, who loved to read celebrity magazines, always shared the gossipy threads of Brent Safer's persona, filaments of stories that were woven into a life fabric that may or may not have been true—it didn't matter to Cameryn because it was always more interesting than her own life. This man had driven the fastest cars, dated the most beautiful entertainers in the world, sailed on yachts, and stayed at a rehab center in Utah designed just for celebrities. And yet he was reduced in death, like every other human. It somehow made her sad.

"What happened to you?" she whispered as Ben pushed the tip of the curved needle through a top portion of the scalp. Cameryn's gaze drifted to the actor's hands; it startled her to realize his nails were manicured, polished as smooth as the inside of a shell. His chest, too, had been waxed so that his skin looked like marble. The soft mix of acoustical guitar and violin had changed to a vocal, and Cameryn suddenly keyed in to the words at the end of the song.

Forever the sand slips through the glass
Love is the thing that eternally lasts
We're fresh when we're young
We wither with age
Live life without borders
And write on your page

She watched Ben clip the thread, unaware, it seemed, of how closely the words echoed the dead man's life.

'Cause even the stars fall from the sky.
They burn as they flame.
They blaze as they die.

She stroked his forearm with a gloved finger. *How did you die? Did someone do this to you? Or is this something you did to yourself?* For the briefest moment she closed her eyes, wishing she could hear an answer the way Lyric swore she could if she would only believe. But instead of ghostly whispers she heard the rumble of Dr. Moore instructing Justin on the disinfection properties of a cleaner called Virex and the clank of metal instruments as they dropped into the sink. No, if the dead were to speak, it would have to be through the evidence they left behind. Clues that she would need to read. She opened her eyes just as Ben finished rethreading the needle.

"Okay, Cammie, now we put the guts back in. Pick up the Hefty bag and hand it to me," he instructed. "Yeah, it's under the table, right by your feet."

Cameryn did as she was told, aware that the bag contained the remains of Brent Safer's dissected organs. It was heavier than she expected, at least fifteen pounds.

"Got it," said Ben as he plucked it from her hands. He

set the bag into Brent Safer's hollowed torso and topped it with the already cut breast plate. "I kind of smoosh it down so it's all even," Ben told her. "Now I'm ready to sew. Watch—I'll teach you a little technique. I clamp the skin together with these towel clips. See? They're a kind of forceps with itty-bitty teeth." He pulled the skin from either side and pinched the edges together with scissors that bent at the end in a kind of clamp. "Then I baste the skin with great big baseball stitches, at least an inch apart."

Cameryn moved closer to Ben's side. Standing on his right, she could hear his gentle grunts as he pushed the needle through. "Human skin is tough," Ben said. She could see a glisten of sweat gathering at the edge of his hair. He pulled down his mask so that it dangled against his chest. "I have to toss the needle when I'm done 'cause they get dull. Same with the scalpels, well, the blades, anyway. They're disposable." The needle popped through the skin as Ben made his way toward the crook in the Y incision. "We still haven't opened up Leather Ed. He's back there in the cooler."

"Oh." She felt a rabbit-kick to her heart. "Well."

"Yeah. I'm telling you, there's some messed-up things going on—first Leather Ed and now these two. This is wild."

At this point Dr. Moore, whose hearing was better

than Cameryn would have guessed, whipped around from the sink to roar, "That's enough, Ben. There will be no discussion of that case with Miss Mahoney. Information concerning that autopsy is off-limits. You know that!"

"Yes, sir. But seeing as Cammie's our friend—"

"All the more reason to keep quiet. I don't want my work thrown out on a technicality." Dr. Moore looked daggers at Ben, as if daring him to speak, but Ben kept on stitching, oblivious to the doctor's cantankerous response. Although Ben meant well, Cameryn couldn't help but feel grateful to the doctor for shutting down the conversation. A queasy feeling spread through her whenever she thought of Kyle. The constant thrum of dread quieted only when she concentrated on other things, like the death of a movie star and the mystery of the clear gel in his lungs. *Focus on that, only that,* she told herself, *and nothing more.*

"So what happens to the junk?" she asked, pointing to the organs in the Hefty bag.

"Huh? Oh . . . the mortician'll take out the bag and dump a bunch of formaldehyde inside and sew it back into the torso. His work'll be finer than mine, though—the stitches'll be a lot closer and neater." As he spoke he looked not at Cameryn or at his handiwork, but at the back of Dr. Moore's head. Justin, too, had turned away from them. She heard the click of the door closing behind her father and the sheriff, who had entered the cooler where the other corpses were kept. It was then Ben made his move. "Cammie," he said, his voice just above a whisper, "Moore's about the rules but I say screw the law."

"Shhh. You'll get fired!" Cameryn shot a look at Dr. Moore, who was now engrossed with scrubbing the Stryker bone saw, explaining the procedure to Justin, who was bent over the sink, asking questions. For a moment, at least, Ben could speak without being overheard.

"Nah, Moore couldn't last a day without me. Listen, we can talk all day about this famous dead guy and his jelly lungs, but I'm more worried about you. Girl, there's a killer on your tail. One of his victims is turning blue in our cooler and I think you got the right to know whatever it is we find out."

"I'm not supposed to know anything," she whispered. The sick feeling twisted in her stomach again as she pictured the body that was less than thirty yards away. A body that had something to do with her. Her mind flashed again to the note, but she shook her head, trying to force the thought away. "Ben, we need to concentrate on *this* case. I've got to leave Leather Ed alone—it's a conflict of interest." She picked up a sponge and mindlessly put it back down again, then did the same with a pair of forceps. How could she explain it so that Ben could understand? Examining Brent Safer made her an expert. Thinking about Leather Ed's corpse made her a victim all over again.

Plunk, plunk, plunk—with a sure hand Ben punctured the skin, leaving a trail of Frankenstein-looking stitches up Brent Safer's chest. Ben eyed Dr. Moore and bent closer still. "All right, have it your way," he murmured. "Remember, all you got to do is ask."

"What are you two whispering about?" Dr. Moore demanded. His fists, balled up, were planted on his hips. Water and blood had sprayed against his apron in a psychedelic pattern of red. He eyed them suspiciously.

"Nothing," she answered, too loud. She felt like she was back in junior high, caught passing notes. It was hard to meet his gaze, but she forced herself to, and then, using her cheeriest voice, she said, "Ben was explaining how he worked in a funeral home. It's amazing. He knows all the angles."

"Yeah, that's right," Ben agreed. "See, I was telling Cammie how I used to work there before I started in this crazy business. Now Cammie, check out that bucket by the sink. I want you to put in about a cup of ProForce floor cleaner in the bucket, fill it with water, and grab a Scotch-Brite sponge, and then I want you to scrub this man down. We got to get all the blood off him."

"You clean the bodies with *floor* cleaner?" she asked, genuinely surprised.

"Uh-huh," Ben replied, and now the familiar smile was back. "It cuts the grease. Fat from the body makes everything kinda slick. After you scrub, I'll show you how to rinse 'em with a hose. I got my own diener hose while the doc's got his. Equal opportunity cleaning."

"Yes, yes, the system is wonderful," Dr. Moore said, seemingly satisfied. "A little less chatter and a little more speed, Ben. We've got a decedent waiting."

Cameryn released a breath, happy she'd smoothed over the rough patch. Stepping away from Brent Safer's remains, she was heading for the yellow plastic bucket when she felt her BlackBerry hum in her pocket. Curious, she pulled it out and looked at the screen, holding it gingerly in her gloved hand. It showed a local number she didn't recognize.

"Hello?" she said. She could hear breathing on the other end, low and rasping. "Hello?"

No answer.

Justin, alert to the sound of her voice, whirled around to look at her.

"Hello?" she asked again.

"Who is it?" Justin demanded.

Cameryn shrugged in reply. She pressed her phone more tightly to her ear. The breathing was still there, but louder. "Who is this?"

"There are no calls in the autopsy suite," Dr. Moore barked. "Tell your little friend you're working and hang up."

And then a voice began to speak to her, disembodied and strangely sweet, a lover's voice, crooning in her ear.

"You shouldn't be in the morgue, Cammie." There was a *tsk*ing sound, three short beats, like the tick of a clock. "What about my note? You're a naughty girl." The breathing began again, in and out, like a bellows.

Cameryn felt her body go rigid, the phone now ice in her hand. Her heart began to beat wildly while her mind registered the voice that she never wanted to hear again.

"I've missed you, my Angel of Death. We belong together. And we will be, very soon. I promise you that."

Justin, sensing what was happening, darted toward her while Cameryn wheeled, dark spots appearing in front of her eyes. Somehow her body had stopped breathing. There were popping noises behind her temples as darkness moved toward her.

"Because you are my *anam cara*. You always have been."

A click, and then the line went dead as her world turned black.

Chapter Six

"I'LL THINK SHE'S finally coming around. Look at her eyelids—they're moving." The voice belonged to Justin. Through her lashes Cameryn could see his face above her, swimming into focus as she tried to adjust her mind. Point by point she could feel sensation return: rough fabric beneath her hands, the buzz of fluorescent lights, the quiet murmur of men's voices crowding overhead. Like puzzle pieces she put the perceptions together. She was in the lobby, laid out on the institutional-style sofa as though she were a corpse on an autopsy table. Light pooled along the top of Dr. Moore's head, his jowls more pronounced as he leaned over her, his blood-spattered apron inches away from her face. Behind him stood Ben and the sheriff. Her father and Justin were kneeling beside her head. Blinking, she pulled herself up to her elbows while the men hovered in a circle overhead, cutting off the light.

"Thank God she's back," her father cried. His strong arms propped her up, but she could feel Justin, too, his hand over hers, rough and warm. Patrick and Justin seemed to be jostling for position, but for now her father had won. His worried eyes searched hers while his hair, usually so controlled, stood straight up from his forehead like feathers. "Baby, are you all right?" he asked. Then the forced smile that she knew meant whatever was happening wasn't good. "It's all okay. You're going to be okay. Just relax now, you're fine."

"What happened?" she croaked. Her throat felt dry. Justin thrust a plastic cup of water toward her. His hands were steady as he pressed it to her lips. Grateful, she drank, as the sheriff said, "You fainted. You would have landed smack on the floor if my deputy hadn't caught you. He grabbed you right before you hit."

"I fainted?" Cameryn felt a hot wave of embarrassment. She'd never, not in her entire life, ever done something so melodramatic. Fainting was something women in old-fashioned movies did. It didn't happen to someone like her, not to a scientist who lived in a world of fact. She began to register the various segments of her body, the way her feet, still encased the paper booties, lay on the arm of the couch. For the briefest of seconds her mind couldn't process *why* it had happened. And then the memory came flooding back and she took in a sharp gasp of air. Kyle. He had called her. Kyle O'Neil knew exactly where she was, which meant he was out there, somewhere, watching her, hunting. She began to shake. "Oh my God," she whispered, her eyes so wide she could feel the strain of her skin. "I remember. Oh my God! Kyle—it was Kyle. *He knows I'm here!*" The shuddering overtook her, rocking her body like waves.

"Get a blanket," her father commanded, and Ben obeyed. "Cameryn, are you sure? Could it have been someone trying to play a joke?"

"No, Dad, I know his voice—it was him!"

"I knew it!" Justin hissed. His hand, balled into a fist, hit the edge of the couch. "I'll kill him. I swear I'll kill him myself."

"I think that'll be *my* job," her father shot back. "Sheriff? Can you trace the call and get a location on that bastard?"

"I'll get right on it," Jacobs said. He held up Cameryn's BlackBerry, which he must have already taken from her when they carried her to the couch. "But I'll lay money that he called her on a disposable phone."

"A what?" Patrick asked.

"A cheap phone you buy and throw out when the minutes are up—you can't track them. My next step is to notify the FBI and the Durango police, but before I do"—he bent close to her, narrowing his eyes—"it's very important that you tell me exactly what he said. Can you do that, Cammie?" Without breaking eye contact he pulled out his pad and pen.

"Now?" Justin snapped. "Why don't you give her a minute?"

"No, Deputy, we do it immediately, while it's still fresh in her mind. Procedure, remember?"

Slowly, painfully, Cameryn repeated the nightmare conversation. Sheriff Jacobs nodded once, twice, three times, then abruptly turned to Dr. Moore. "Would it be okay if I used your office to make the call? It'll be more private from there, Doc. If we've got any chance of tracing this wacko I need to move now."

"Be my guest," Dr. Moore replied. Suddenly, Cameryn registered the doctor's hand on the top of her head, patting her as though she were a child. It was the first time he'd ever touched her. When she looked up into his gruff face she saw his eyes glisten with emotion. "I have every confidence that your father, the deputy, and the sheriff will keep you safe," he told her. He swallowed and his Adam's apple bobbed somewhere beneath the folds of his neck. "Add my name to the list. I'd never let anyone hurt my star protégée."

"Thanks, Dr. Moore."

"Now go home and get some rest."

"But Joseph Stein . . . the autopsy . . ." she protested.

"We'll manage." He turned his gaze to her father, then to Justin. "Keep her safe. I've already seen what Kyle O'Neil is capable of. I never want to see his handiwork again."

"Mammaw, I'm fine," Cameryn moaned. "Stop hovering!"

"You call it hoverin', do ya?" her grandmother snapped as she paced around the kitchen table where Cameryn sat. "Hoverin', when there's a madman out there looking to snatch you away! Hoverin', when the next time Kyle O'Neil shows up it might be in person, and then what will you do?" Her tone shifted ever so slightly as she added, "Now I'd like you to eat. Today's been a shock."

Sighing, Cameryn propped her head on her hand. Steam from the bowl wafted to her face. Although it smelled delicious, her stomach closed against it. "I'm not hungry."

"Of course you are. Take a bite."

"Mammaw, not every problem is solved by food."

The normally soft Irish lilt her grandmother spoke with, a legacy from her childhood in Ireland, turned crisp as she said, "This trouble circles back to you being around all that death. I've said all along forensics is wrong and now my words have come home to roost."

In a red Valentine sweater, her earlobes elongated by heavy plastic heart-shaped earrings, Mammaw looked like the majority of Silverton grandmothers, with her square face crowned by a wreath of short, white hair. But Mammaw was different from the other women. She was an Irish force of nature.

"Please," Cameryn begged. "Don't start."

"I'm only saying you should forget this autopsy nonsense and dedicate your life to becoming a *real* doctor." As always, her grandmother reminded Cameryn of a chicken hunting grain. Peck, peck, peck—her words nibbled away at Cameryn, a sharp tapping against her skull. Groaning softly, Cameryn dropped her head into her hands.

"Are you listening, girl? Your career choice is nothing short of crazy."

"I'm not crazy. The voices told me I'm *supposed* to go into forensics."

"So it's sarcasm now, is it? You think my concerns are a joke."

Cameryn and her mammaw glared at one another for a moment until her grandmother did an unexpected thing. Dropping back her head, she let out a great guffaw, a deep laugh that shook Cameryn up as much as anything. "I never have to worry how Irish you are, Cameryn Mahoney. You're as pigheaded as they come. Now do your grandmother a favor and eat. For me."

"All right, all right, I give up. No dessert, though."

"Whatever you say."

Sighing, Cameryn picked up a spoon and took a sip of stew. It burned her mouth but after the third bite she had to admit she felt better, and by the time she took the last swallow the knot inside had loosened. Dr. Moore had been right—home was the place she needed to be, wrapped up in its tacky, snug security, with pink and red carnations on a round kitchen table in a vase shaped like a heart. Today the walls were laced with cutouts featuring cherubs floating on ridiculously small wings. Handmade Valentines from Cameryn's preschool days had been stuck to the refrigerator with magnets shaped like lips. Her grandmother bustled about, trying to look busy, but Cameryn could sense there was more she wanted to say. After wiping a spot on the counter for a third time, Mammaw drew in a sharp breath and said, "Lyric came by earlier—she wanted to know about the case. While she was here she told me some interesting news about you and Justin. That Lyric is a talkative girl."

"News?" Cameryn felt her internal alarm register at full alert.

"News." Her grandmother tossed the dishcloth onto the counter and crossed her arms over her chest, obscuring a large embroidered heart. "And don't be going after your friend just because she was kind enough to bring me up to speed on the goings-on in your life. She claims to have known all along you and the deputy were going to be together through some kind of spirit mumbo jumbo, but even I can see you and Justin have been eyeing each other for months. Is he thinking of you as his girlfriend?"

"Not exactly," she replied, making a mental note to throttle Lyric the next time she saw her.

"What does 'not exactly' mean? Exactly."

Shrugging, Cameryn chewed on the edge of her lip. "He said he liked me. It's no big deal."

She knew how her grandmother felt about Justin, that she was fond of him but he was almost twenty-two and twenty-two-year-old men were not to be trusted.

"And your father? What does he have to say?"

"Dad's been cool with Justin for a while. Um, you know, maybe I will have some dessert after all," Cameryn said in a desperate attempt to deflect her grandmother's steely gaze. "Even though I'm a disaster in the kitchen I think I might give cooking another shot. Since Irish is my heritage and all." Her voice trailed off. She could see by her grandmother's expression it was useless.

"Although I still feel he's too old, the fact that you're in danger means it might be a good time to have a more mature person offering you protection. But if you do enter these waters you must be cautious, Cameryn. Things can happen."

"Mammaw!"

"There are certain pitfalls that can come with dating someone older. What I'm trying to say . . ." Mammaw hesitated and then, clearly uncomfortable, said, "You *do* understand the position of the church in these matters." Red flamed at the tips of her ears. She was actually blushing.

"All he said was that he *liked* me," Cameryn cried. "I'm not getting married or anything!"

"These days marriage and—the rest—don't necessarily go together."

"Mammaw!"

"The older one in the relationship always has the power."

"Will you stop! We—he's not like that. I cannot believe we're having this conversation. I'd rather talk about Kyle killing me."

"What you have with Justin poses a different kind of danger, girl."

Now it was Cameryn whose skin flushed. She could feel the warmth spread from her cheeks down her neck until it touched the skin on her chest. "Look, I'm not planning to do anything Father Pat wouldn't approve of, if that's what you mean."

"Good," Mammaw said, her voice once again crisp. "Now, here's your Irish raisin cake, which I made *without* the whiskey. I'm glad of it since I hear a truck in the driveway. The deputy's truck, if I'm not mistaken."

Cameryn jumped out of her seat as she registered the familiar sound of Justin's engine. "He's here?"

"It appears so."

"What if he heard us? I will *die* if he heard what you were saying."

"Don't be silly, girl, no one has ears that good. Besides, he should know that I'll be watching."

"Mammaw, you need to go." With a hand on each of her grandmother's shoulders Cameryn pushed her mammaw toward the living room. "Turn on the TV or sew something."

"Offer him some food, Cammie. Men are always hungry," her grandmother called over her shoulder.

"Yeah. 'Bye." Cameryn's grandmother had just disappeared when she heard his footsteps. It annoyed her to realize how her body turned against her. Her heart skipped beats as he trod up their back steps, stomping twice to shake off the snow. This reaction to Justin's presence was absurd. How many times had they shared the same space, working forensic cases side by side? Hadn't they just gone to the autopsy together? But tonight seemed different somehow, probably because of her grandmother's pointed conversation and the images that conversation had stirred up. *Get a grip,* she commanded as Justin's tall, lanky form loomed dark behind the gauzy kitchen curtain. Three sharp raps announced his arrival.

"Hey," Cameryn said, opening the door.

"Hi, Cammie. I thought I'd stop by and see how you were doing."

"I'm fine. Come on in. Sit."

Justin peeled off his coat and hung it on the back of a chair, then straddled it as if it were a bar stool, while she sat in a chair next to him. He'd changed into different jeans and a navy cotton turtleneck that brought out the blue in his eyes. Thick lashes heightened the color—doll's eyes, her mammaw called them. He placed his hand on hers and squeezed. "Besides checking up on you, I'm here on business. Kyle used a disposable phone, just like Jacobs thought, so there's no way to trace it. The scary part is that he got close. Kyle"—he spat the name—"knew you were in the morgue. Which means he must have followed you."

The warmth inside her vanished. "I don't want to talk about it," she said, pulling her hand free.

"Typical, evasive Cammie," he said, his eyes locking on to hers. "Don't talk about it and it doesn't exist, right?" His tone carried the slightest hint of chastisement.

"Can't we just pretend that there isn't a killer after me? Just for a couple of hours," she begged. "Please, Justin, I really need the mental break. I want to . . . forget."

He sighed. "Okay. No more hard truths tonight. You do look really tired."

"Great. That means I look awful. Tired is a euphemism for gross." She tried to smooth her hair with her fingers but knew it was useless. Stupidly, she hadn't bothered to change since she'd gotten home, or done anything to clean herself up. *Perfect*, she thought. The only comfort she had was that Justin had seen her look worse.

"I didn't say that," he answered, seemingly amused. "You know you're gorgeous. I just think maybe I'm being selfish, dropping by when it's already"—he glanced at his watch—"eight o'clock on a school night, which sounds incredibly weird when I say it out loud."

"Mammaw told me I don't have to go to class tomorrow if I don't want to and I've decided I'm sleeping in. I already texted Lyric so she won't pull me out of bed at the crack of dawn. Stay. Distract me from my misery."

When he looked doubtful, she said, "A true friend would think of something to cheer me up. So . . . what do you want to do?" She looked around her kitchen, suddenly realizing their house wasn't exactly equipped to entertain anyone under the age of fifty. Here, encased in a kitchen full of cherubs, she saw with fresh eyes how old-fashioned their lives appeared. "I've got cards. Or do you like games?" she asked, feeling lamer by the minute.

He raked his fingers through his too-long hair. "How about a movie?"

She shook her head. "I don't think that's a good idea. We've only got one television and it's in the living room and my grandmother's in there," she said, keeping her voice low.

"Ahh." His eyes twinkled. "And she doesn't like me."

"No, she likes you," Cameryn clarified. "She doesn't *trust* you."

He gave a wicked grin. "Wise woman."

What was that supposed to mean? Cameryn flushed as Justin closed the distance between them. "Kidding," he told her. "Actually, I planned ahead. On the off chance you invited me to hang out I brought two choices of movies, although from the shadows under your eyes I doubt you'll stay awake for either one." Reaching around, he pulled two DVD cases from an inside fold of his jacket. "Comedy or"—he held up a second plastic square—"action movie with exploding guts. What's your pleasure?"

"Comedy," she said. "I'm definitely in the mood to laugh."

"Excellent. Let's ask your mammaw to join us."

Cameryn waited a beat before saying, "You're not serious. You want my *grandmother* to watch a movie with us? Why?"

"Because even though you've decided that all you can handle is friendship, I'm looking ahead. If we're going to be together then winning over your mammaw and your pop is on my agenda." He wagged his eye-brows. "Okay?"

As they settled into the couch, a foot of upholstery respectfully between them, her grandmother watched, eagle-eyed. She'd been pleased by the invitation, Cameryn could tell, and Cameryn marveled at how effortless Justin made it all seem. He'd chatted up her grandmother as if they were the best of friends, and as the opening credits rolled she felt Justin move closer. In some ways his presence soothed her. Light flickered across his face as the scenes changed, and from beneath her lashes Cameryn watched Justin instead of the movie. There was no denying how handsome he was—the sharp juts of his cheekbones changing as the reflection slid across the planes of his face, hair curling softly against his neck, his shoulders broad. In the background she heard the creak from her grandmother's chair interrupted by quiet bursts of laughter.

The edges of the screen blurred as she tried to pay attention, but the dialogue wove through her mind, musical notes tied to language instead of words. She floated in this world like a bubble, drifting from one scene to another until suddenly she was back in the autopsy room. But this time it was Kyle on the table and Justin who held the knife. The blade gleamed at Kyle's shoulder but Cameryn yelled for Justin to stop.

At that moment Kyle's eyes snapped open. His icy hand grabbed her arm—

"Wake up, Cammie. It's just a dream. You're only dreaming."

It wasn't Kyle's hand, but Justin's, that held hers. Blinking, she looked over to the empty rocking chair. "Your mammaw gave up," Justin answered before she could think to ask the question. "She went to bed, but not before she reminded me that your pop was on the way."

"What—what time is it?" she asked thickly.

"Ten thirty."

"Wow. I can't believe I fell asleep. And you *let* me?" She rose up from his shoulder. "Why didn't you wake me up?"

"I let you sleep because you needed it. You're heavier than you look, though. My arm is completely numb."

Cameryn punched his shoulder. "Stop!"

"I'm serious," he laughed, but this time he caught her wrist as she tried to hit him again. "Listen, I should go. It's late and your pop won't like it if he finds out his daughter slept with me. *Ouch!*"

Switching to her left hand she caught him in his upper arm.

"Man, you hit like a guy. No, I cannot let you do that again," he said. He grabbed both wrists.

Trapped, she looked up at him. His hair was tousled

as though he'd been sleeping, too. She was aware of the illumination from the television, of the way their breathing cadenced together, of how close his face was next to hers so that she could feel his heat. All traces of playfulness vanished as he released her right hand and touched the bottom of her lip. She felt herself shiver. Her hand rose up to touch his cheek, stroking it with her fingertips.

When his lips brushed hers it was sweet, tender. "Is this okay?" he whispered.

She nodded.

"Because I can wait, Cammie."

"I know you can. But I can't." This time it was Cameryn who kissed him, and she realized this was what she'd wanted. Death and fear faded away as she drank him in. Justin. Her Justin. It was the letting go that felt so good as she allowed herself this single light in the darkness. *No more running*, she promised herself. *No more thinking, no more evasion. Just . . . being.* As he pulled back, light caught the scar on the edge of his chin, as thin as a thread.

"I've always wondered. How did you get that?" she asked, touching it gently.

"Now *that's* a story. But not one for tonight. It's late, Cammie. You should go to bed and get some rest."

"You're leaving?"

He sighed deeply. "If your father finds me on the

couch with you he might shoot first and ask questions later."

"I don't want you to leave."

He grinned and pulled her close. "You have no idea how good that sounds. I can be here tomorrow when my shift's over."

"I'd like that," she answered softly.

"Then I'm going to say good night." He kissed her again, harder this time, and Cameryn felt her heart kick in her chest. "No, stay here," he said when she attempted to rise from the couch with him. "I'll lock the door on my way out. Sweet dreams, Cammie. Promise me you'll think only good thoughts tonight."

"Promise you'll come back as soon as you can."

He shot her a crooked grin. "Deal."

Muffled footsteps echoed in her kitchen, followed by the quiet click of the lock. Happy, she hugged herself as the slash of headlights slid across the window, bright as stars. With a conscious choice she had chosen to leap into life. Death, in all its forms, had been left behind.

Chapter Seven

THIS TIME HER dream was a good one. She was with Justin. The two of them were tucked into a small canoe on a deep mountain lake surrounded by sunflowers that grew right to the water's edge, like a ring of fire. Justin pushed the oars while Cameryn watched the muscles strain beneath his skin. Wind whipped at his hair. "Do you want to keep going?" he called against the wind. Now he was rowing toward a ribbon of water, only ten feet in length, an umbilical cord of blue connecting the lake with the ocean. With another deep stroke he warned, "The ocean is more dangerous. Are you sure you want to go on?" Waves crashed into the side of their rowboat but she was not afraid. In the distance she saw the tip of a whale's undulating tail, and she smiled happily and said yes. . . .

Something from beyond was reaching into her dream. Reluctant, she resisted the pull to the surface of consciousness, fighting hard to stay under with Justin and the whitecapped waves. It was no use. The noise came again, a note from an instrument, a small ring, the flute from a wind chime. Was she in class? No, she could feel the pillow beneath her head and the comforter clutched to her chin. She felt the plastic nose of Rags, her stuffed dog, pressed into her side. Her eyelids fluttered open and Justin disappeared into the ocean as though he were a mist. Groaning, she realized she was in her own bedroom, alone, with only Rags for company.

Light from the full moon flooded her bedroom so that she could see the outline of her lamp, and beyond that her computer with her screen saver morphing into geometric shapes. She'd left her computer on again—her dad would chew her out if he saw that, convinced as he was that every bad thing happened when Microsoft Outlook was left open. No matter, she would reboot in the morning. Yawning long and deep, she stretched her arms over her head until she gave a tiny, inadvertent squeak. Rolling onto her side, she looked at her clock. Red numbers glowed in the darkness in electronic blocks: 3:03 A.M. Groaning again, she wondered if she could ever get back to sleep. With her arm flung across her eyes, she tried to follow the wisps of her dream but moments later she knew it was no good. Emotions, once suppressed by sleep, rose up inside to crash together.

Justin and Kyle. Light and dark, good and evil—two divergent streams flowed into her conscience. It wasn't hard for her to select which emotional channel she wanted to follow. The trick was to silence the other by submerging it back to the depths. But *aman cara* washed to the forefront, and she felt herself begin to shake. *Stop!* she told herself fiercely. Think about Justin. She could do this—it was just a matter of choice. Pulling her comforter to the bridge of her nose, she commanded herself to focus on the good. She would not allow herself to hear the whisper of Kyle's voice, to picture him out there, watching, waiting. No, she would relive the kiss. The kiss and nothing more.

She squeezed her eyelids together as hard as she could. If she concentrated she could almost feel the sensation of Justin's mouth against hers. Yes, that was the thought she wanted. She savored the feel of his cheek pressed into her forehead, the prickles from his five-o'clock shadow against her skin, and the way he'd wound his hand through her hair before he'd said his last good-bye—yes, these were the images she could replay forever.

Smiling, she remembered Lyric's squeal when Cameryn delivered the news. With the phone cupped in her hand, Cameryn had whispered the story from the kitchen's land line, aware that her father would be home at any moment but intent on sharing with her closest friend. When she'd finished Lyric had cried, "I knew it! I knew it! This is karma—I told you from the very first day you'd end up together. I *told* you I had a feeling! All those times you were in denial of my powers. Take that, doubter!"

Now, Cameryn found herself chuckling quietly at the thought of her friend's over-the-top reaction. Lyric, with her crystals, had been on to something after all.

As her lids slid open she studied the pattern the moonlight made on her ceiling, trying to remember when things between herself and Justin had changed, realizing there hadn't been an exact moment—it was more of an awareness of what had always been. In the same way the lake of her dream had turned into the ocean, her feelings had grown bigger, more precarious. Dangerous, the dream-Justin had said. The perfect word.

But could it last? In the autumn she would move to Durango to go to school while he remained in Silverton. Then again, they each had a car and weekends could be worked out easily, perhaps meeting at Purgatory since it was almost in the middle. *Stop!* she commanded. *You haven't even graduated from high school. One kiss doesn't mean you're a forever couple! Get a grip, Cam-*

mie! He might change his mind tomorrow and decide she was too young after all.

Even as she said it to herself she knew it was a lie. Whatever this was, it was real. Justin. Justin and Cameryn. As though she were moving through her rosary beads she touched that idea over and over again, allowing herself to become accustomed to its feel. Cameryn and Justin. Another smile tugged at the corners of her mouth and she sighed, ready to return to her dreams. Her eyes were just beginning to close when she heard it again—the soft two-note chime that had awakened her in the first place. It came from the computer, signaling that another e-mail had arrived. Spam, she thought, and hopped out of bed to turn it off. Sleeping would be hard enough without interruptions, no matter how small. Dancing through the cold, she dropped into her chair and moved the mouse, which caused the screen saver to vanish, revealing the biology paper she'd been working on. She maximized her in-box. Two new e-mails had arrived since she'd gone to bed. Who would send her e-mails at three A.M.?

It took a moment for her mind to comprehend. The mouse froze in her hand.

Each message bore the name Kyle O'Neil. Her brain, her heart, everything seemed to stop as she stared at the single word on the subject line and its reflection in the message below. She couldn't catch her breath as she read:

Angel

The letter-shaped icons shimmered in pale yellow.

The beginning of the message screamed at her in cobalt blue:

This is my last hope for reaching you. I'm begging . . .

Her eyes snapped to the second e-mail:

Angel,

I know they took your BlackBerry and you keep your computer on. Please, open this letter . . .

She stared for a minute, or five, or ten—she had no idea, because it seemed as if time itself dissolved and there was nothing but the screen and her body.

He had found her. Again.

Angel

She should go and wake her father. Even though it was the middle of the night she knew she should call the sheriff. Justin would want to be the first person she turned to—yes, he should be the one. But she found she couldn't move. Cold air wrapped up her legs and slithered up her arm like a snake as she stared, trying to push down the terror that welled inside. The words branded her soul. Closing her eyes, she hoped for a moment that this was part of the dream, but when she looked at the screen they were still there. The words had not moved.

Angel

And then something inside burst through the frozen dam. Her blood rocketed as she read the word again and again. Angel. How *dare* he call her that! This inhuman machine who would kill without mercy, who was now tracking her down like prey. Why was he doing this? Protocol vanished. As if her hand had a mind of its own she snatched the mouse and double-clicked the first message. It read:

This is my last hope for reaching you. I'm begging you to hear me. Please, write back and let me explain. I am not the monster you think. I'm at my computer, waiting. I know you won't believe me, but what I am writing is true. I love you.

Kyle

And then the next:

Angel

I know you keep your computer on. Please, open this letter—it's the only way we can speak. If I wanted to hurt you, I could have. Easily. But that is not my plan. There are things to say. I can help you if you let me. Write back.

Love,

Kyle

Her blood pounded so hard she could hear her own pulse threading through her neck. She would not allow herself to think. Her fingers spilled rage as they flew across her keyboard.

What is wrong *with you? Why can't you leave me alone!?! I want you to leave me alone! I'm asking you to go away. Forever. Turn yourself in!*

Not allowing herself to think she hit send. Her father would be furious, but it wasn't Patrick who was in Kyle's sights. She was the target; everyone else only orbited on the periphery. Images of her life tumbled, then focused, and she saw herself clearly as the victim she had become. The picture of herself made her sick to her stomach. When had she become so weak? Kyle had overtaken her. He had infected her life and she was going to exorcise him herself. This was a battle between the two of them. Kyle and Cameryn, alone in the dark, while Silverton slept.

Chewing her fingernail, she stared at the screen until she heard the familiar chime.

If I could leave you alone I would have long ago. Do you remember the night when I took you to the cemetery? How can I make you understand—I changed that night. I am so sorry about the shed. You saw me out of control. You witnessed a side of me I fight to keep in check. For a long time I believed that there was no way for me to restrain that part of myself. But I now realize that you have changed me. Will you listen?

She was no longer cold. Two red splotches burned on her cheeks.

Listen? she wrote, her fingers flying. *You killed Brad*

Oakes. You killed Leather Ed. I'm guessing you killed Brent Safer and Joseph Stein. Turn yourself in and you can get help. You are sick.

A moment later the computer chimed again, two frail notes:

Leather Ed died before I got there. I did not kill the movie star or the producer. But if you will talk to me, I will tell you who killed them. Cammie, you can see my mind in what I left behind.

Her fingers flew as if they were possessed:

You are a murderer! You are a liar!

This time the message took longer to receive.

I came back for you, Cammie. You have to believe me when I say that they will never find me—you have to understand that. It would be easier for everyone if you would do what I am asking you to do. No one else will get hurt. I give you my word. Talking through e-mail is painfully slow, so I've set up a chat room for us—the password is An6el1. Meet me there.

The cold fear was back, spreading through her with a frozen kind of terror. *Hurt.* She focused on the word. Who would he hurt if she refused him? Faster this time, she wrote:

What do you mean when you say hurt? Who are you talking about?

A moment later she heard the malevolent ring. This time the message contained only a single name.

Justin.

She stared at the screen. It wasn't possible. Kyle was still a teenager and Justin was a man armed with a gun, trained by the police in New York. Justin was smarter than anyone she knew. There should be no way Kyle could ever get to him. Her head thrummed all the right words, but something wasn't connecting inside. It was her heart. The link between her head and her heart had severed like a thread snapped in two.

What if she was wrong? What if something happened to Justin because of her? With fingers shaking so hard they could barely touch the keys, she curled her palm against her desktop, ready to type. Her mind, though, had gone blank. She looked at the last message and felt the world drop out beneath her. Justin. Because of her Justin might be harmed or worse. The bravado she'd been riding slipped away as she tried to comprehend this unexpected change in the game. The computer chimed again. This time he'd sent a message out of turn.

Justin. Justin. Justin. Justin. Justin. Justin. Justin. Justin. Justin. Justin.

She tried to cry out her father's name, but her voice seemed to gurgle in her throat. "Dad." It was barely a whisper.

Once, and then again, she tried with all the force

she could muster to push air between her lips but the word came out in a faint croak. She had to concentrate until her mouth would work again. "Dad. *Dad!*" she cried, thankful her body was finally responding, grateful that help was going to come.

"Cammie!" her father cried. "Cammie—what is it?"

"I need you!"

Under the computer's glare she listened to the footsteps running toward her. "Hurry," she cried with a final strangled sob. "Please hurry!"

The door to her room flew open and her father ran to her, his face twisted in panic. "What is it, Cammie? What's wrong? Good Lord, what are you doing up in the middle of the night? You had me scared to death!"

With a shaking finger, she pointed to her screen.

He walked close enough to read and then he stopped. Understanding dawned as he looked at the screen. In the computer's half-light his skin appeared gray, his hair a tousled mat of white, his pajamas, striped cotton, rumpled from sleep. She could see her father blanch as his eyes traced the words written on the screen, his mouth open, his muscles tense as horror registered on his face. "Where is your phone?" he asked her through stiff lips.

"I don't have it. The sheriff took it today when—"

"Ma!" he bellowed. "Bring me a phone. I'm in Cammie's room and I need it. *Now!*"

She could hear her grandmother's feet thumping loudly as they ran for the cordless phone kept on a table at the end of the hall. "I'm coming, Patrick. What's happened?"

Part of Mammaw's red and white flannel nightgown was balled up in one hand so that she could run without tripping. Patrick took the phone Mammaw thrust at him and hit the numbers as though he would punch them right through the handset.

"John?" her father cried. "Sorry to wake you but he's after my daughter again. Yes, Kyle O'Neil. I need you here now—bring the FBI and the CBI and the CIA and any other gun you've got. I want an army!"

A pause, and then the ice blue eyes settled on Cameryn's. As he spoke, Patrick's face contorted: panic, fear, pain, anger—one emotion replacing the other, each more intense than the last. "Yes." His nod was sharp. "Yes—on her computer. He's crazy, John. He's crazy and he's watching." His voice broke as he pinched the bridge of his nose between his thumb and his forefinger. "And wake up the deputy, too. It's not just Cammie anymore that he wants. Now he's got Justin in his sights."

Chapter Eight

HER GRANDMOTHER MUST be in her heaven, Cameryn thought. Bustling about the Mahoney home with coffee, Mammaw hovered and fussed over the three men and the lone woman crowded inside Cameryn's small bedroom along with Cameryn and her father. Cameryn, who had changed into sweats, clutched Rags to her chest as she leaned cross-legged against her headboard. Now that she had finished answering their questions she could watch the people huddle around her computer, their brows furrowed as they read and reread Kyle's e-mails. For now they were letting her be.

". . . check out the IRC and follow the IP address . . ."

". . . hunt down that password . . . maybe contact DHS . . ."

The window had been cracked so that a stream of cool air filtered into her increasingly stuffy room. Through a gap in the curtains, she watched the full moon. Sallow as wax, it balanced on the mountain's tip like a ball on the nose of a seal. Although she had barely slept she was too full of adrenaline to feel tired, and so, alert, her thoughts bounced from one conversation to another. It was strange, this odd sense of apartness. People talked *about* her, not *to* her—even Justin stood at a distance, consumed with questions about cyber tracking. She didn't mind. The one person whom she'd been most anxious to see was here, and as she watched him stare at the screen with his fierce, unyielding concentration, she felt—not calm, but a kind of acceptance. What mattered most had already happened. Justin was safe. That fact allowed her to breathe again.

". . . what I figured, he got an IP that's nontraceable," Justin said through clenched teeth. "This punk knows what he's doing." His fists tightened and released with every word, as though he were siphoning anger through his fingers. The gun he never wore off duty had been tucked into the back waistband of his jeans. She could see it bulge beneath his green Hudson Valley Community College tee shirt.

Her grandmother drifted by. "Would you like something, girl?" She patted Cameryn vaguely.

"No, thanks," Cameryn replied as her grandmother, sensing an empty coffee cup nearby, floated away.

They're not going to catch him.

She seemed to understand this truth before anyone else in the room. It was as though she were watching a paramedic desperately trying to shock life back into a corpse when it was clear the person was gone. Dead, Cameryn knew, was dead. She could tell by the way Sheriff Jacobs stood that he understood this, too. He leaned against the wall with his arms crossed over his chest, his hard eyes watching the action from behind polished lenses. No, it was Justin and her father who were trying to control the universe, as if by sheer mental force they could bend time and space and catch Kyle O'Neil. Their two heads bent toward the computer, so close to each other they almost touched, the white hair brushing against the dark.

A thin man from the FBI and a heavyset woman from the Colorado Bureau of Investigation spoke to each other in a code of letters followed by a perplexing string of numbers. "Negative," the woman said and sighed.

"What's *negative*? Why can't you *find* him?" her father demanded, standing up to his full height. Like Cameryn and her mammaw, he'd changed from his pajamas, but unlike Mammaw, who'd traded her nightgown for her Sunday best, her father had thrown on old Dockers and a sweatshirt. His hair was uncombed and his feet were bare. "It's been over an hour—that animal threatened my daughter!"

The FBI agent was named Andrew Thliveris. A man in his forties with silvered hair and dark eyes, he'd arrived in the middle of the night wearing a suit, something no native of Silverton would ever do. But his voice was casual. "Call me Andrew," he'd told them. "Thliveris is a mouthful." Now when he spoke his tone was measured, patient. "I understand how upsetting this is, but it's not that easy."

"You say that but you've got his e-mail address *right there*!" Patrick exclaimed, jabbing his finger at the screen.

"I'm afraid Kyle O'Neil's been warchalking."

"What the heck does *that* mean?"

With his left hand Andrew loosened the knot of his tie, a solid red with a single blue stripe. "It means he piggybacked his machine onto a random unprotected connection. It means he's using someone else's Internet linkage to communicate with your daughter. We narrowed it down to a class C network originating from Fort Lewis College."

"You got it narrowed down to the Fort?" Justin asked. For a second his face came alive around the eyes, but the excitement vanished when Andrew said, "No—wait!" He pressed his palms toward the floor. "I'm sorry, but O'Neil's gone." It took a moment for the words to sink in.

"We traced the origin point to the college library but we got there too late."

"Jesus, Mary, and Joseph," Mammaw murmured. Her hand rose to her throat as she sagged into an empty folding chair, one of three that had been placed around the perimeter of the room. Justin dropped his head back and stared at the ceiling.

So it is a fact now—he got away. The words swirled around Cameryn and above her like flakes of snow that chilled her to the bone. For a moment no one spoke, but she could hear her grandmother murmuring prayers, a steady current against the silence.

"Look, I know this is hard," Andrew said to everyone in the room, "but don't get discouraged. O'Neil's showing himself—that's the important thing. The more he contacts Cameryn the better our chances of finding him. Don't you agree?" he asked, directing this comment to the CBI agent.

"Absolutely," the woman answered. "A tracer route, which is what we had to do to get the Fort Lewis hit, takes time. If we can keep this guy talking we can tighten the net. We'll get him."

"How?" Patrick asked. A single word, it seemed as loud as a gunshot. Her grandmother stopped praying in order to eye Andrew.

"Well, a lot of that depends on your girl here." Andrew smiled, showing teeth.

"What is it, exactly, you're wanting?" Mammaw demanded.

Cameryn had the sense that Andrew had been waiting for this opening all along. He came and stood by the foot of her bed and rested his hand on her bedpost, his thick wedding band flashing in the light. His tone was low, his words reassuring as he leaned in toward her. "We can have an agent pose as Cameryn, but I don't think they'll be able to fool this guy for long. Kyle knows you. He understands your style. So, if you agree to continue talking to him, I can assure you that we'll monitor your every communication. You will be completely safe."

"No!" Justin roared.

Ignoring him, Andrew said, "If you help us, we have a much better chance of getting O'Neil. You can draw this guy out. Will you do it?"

She wanted to curl away from the terrifying question, but it wasn't just her life at stake now. There was Justin's. When she nodded it seemed as though the room erupted. She refused to look at Justin, her father, her grandmother. Instead she kept her eyes locked on Andrew's, blocking the cacophony of voices that demanded her to stop, that refused to allow her to do what she knew was necessary. The conversation had narrowed. It was between Andrew and Cameryn.

"How far are you willing to go to catch him? It's really up to you." He moved so close they almost touched. "How far, Cammie?"

And then, in a voice so low only Andrew could hear it, Cameryn replied, "I'll go as far as it takes."

"No *way*. Tell me you're not serious," Lyric demanded as she stretched across Cameryn's bed on her stomach. She wore a loose caftan covered with huge, multicolored polka dots and a pair of jeans that flared at the knees. Her nails had been painted neon yellow. "Your dad is letting you be the bait in this little government trap? Get *out*!"

"I'm not bait," Cameryn argued. "Not exactly."

"It sounds to me like you're the carrot on the end of a stick, the fly in the web, the honey for the bear, the chum in the water . . . I think I'm running out of colorful metaphors."

"Look, every electronic device is being monitored and the agents are hiding practically in plain sight. I'm perfectly safe. They even gave me my BlackBerry back." She held it up and wagged it in front of her friend's face. "See?

"Fabulous." Lyric sighed, long and loud. "The security fairies *promise* you'll be safe, so no worries, right? Nothing could *possibly* go wrong if the government's involved!" She rolled over like a sea lion and placed a plump arm across her eyes, as if to block out the afternoon light.

Lyric had arrived at the Mahoney home the minute school was out, clumping up the stairs twice as fast as usual, the echo of her boots deafening against the wooden treads. At first, Lyric had babbled a list of half-truths that had already blazed through the hallways of Silverton High, her kohl-rimmed eyes wide with excitement. Her mood had darkened, momentarily, when Cameryn calmly explained what had actually happened during the night, but, true to form, she was determined to bring things back to normal. Stories of Adam were wedged between tirades against Tiffany, who "wished she were being stalked so she could be the center of the world again," and who had been acting "like she knew everything about Kyle." Lyric's conversation became a runaway car, filled with bumps, swerves, and screeching brakes, until she veered back to the FBI and asked about security and if that meant everything Cameryn did was being watched.

"So are they, like, making notes about me right now?" Lyric asked. She picked at a loose thread on the bedspread, winding it around her fingertip, then pulled it away so that it left a tiny coil.

"Yep," Cameryn answered. "Every person, every call, every time."

"And if I text you they're going to have a record of everything I write?"

"Uh-huh."

"How long is that going to go on? Because I don't exactly want my words put in some file where the government can see. It would actually bother me more except for the fact that my ramblings aren't actually interesting enough for anyone to read them more than once."

"I know, I know," Cameryn said, trying to give the impression she was listening. The computer monitor pulled her with its own gravity. From her desk she had a view of her screen, the BlackBerry propped against its side, and the cordless phone she'd set next to them. Her window offered a vantage point from which she could survey the street. It was quiet out there as well, as if the street, too, were holding its breath. The trees, stripped of leaves, were still, and the branches cut sharp shadows against the snow. Few cars drove by. Once she saw her neighbor's face framed in an upstairs window before she vanished, snapping the curtains shut.

All day long Cameryn had been on full alert, edgy, and yet . . . nothing had happened. The chat room remained silent, even when she'd tried to contact Kyle exactly the way Andrew told her to. She placed her foot on the rung of her chair and watched her BlackBerry for any sign of life. It seemed to stare back with a blank face. Cameryn chewed on the edge of her finger as she checked into the chat room once again, nodding for Lyric in what she hoped were the right places.

". . . your grandmother said to cheer you up and

I told her I was the master of 'fun shui.' I know I'm great for giggles and grins but it's a little crazy being locked up in a room like this. Maybe we should get out of here."

"I'm not supposed to. Oh, but I get to go see Dr. Moore tomorrow," Cameryn said, suddenly excited. "My dad's taking me—well, my dad plus a police escort. Moore wants me to go over the jelly-in-the-lungs report, so I'll be free, at least for a little while. I'm glad the media's all over Brent Safer and Joseph Stein. I'd hate it if they caught wind of my little drama. That's the last thing I'd want." She shuddered as she looked at her screen. Still nothing.

"This waiting thing is kind of nuts." Lyric's feet now hung off the edge of the bed like two anchors. They started to jiggle so that the heels of her boots clacked together, a sure sign, Cameryn knew, that she was nervous. "What are you going to do about classes? I mean, are you coming back?"

"My dad's talking to the principal right now. If they catch Kyle today . . ." She didn't finish the thought. Outside, she watched Justin's squad car drift by. It slowed, then moved on, like a shark circling its prey.

"And there he goes again," Cameryn said. "I don't believe this."

"Who?"

"Justin. He just made, like, his fiftieth pass by my

house. He's going to burn up the entire Silverton police gas budget if he keeps it up and—wait a second."
She squinted, then stood, pulling back the gauzy inner curtain. "Oh, no. He's backing up. A-a-a-n-d he's
parking, which means he's coming in. This just gets
better and better."

Lyric struggled halfway up, leaning on her elbows.
The red swaths in her hair looked not so much like
rubies as bloodstains, and from this angle Cameryn
could see the blonde margin of her roots. "I thought
Justin coming here would be a good thing."

"Normally, yes. It's just he—well, Justin isn't happy
about the plan. About me helping with the sting. *Upset*
might be the best word. Or maybe *freaked out*."

"Big surprise. I'm not happy about the plan, either,
but you're not exactly listening to me. So, should I
come back another time?"

Through the window, Cameryn tried to read the expression on Justin's face. His jaw was set in a way
that made her nervous, as did the erect way he held
himself, as though he'd been filled with some kind of
energy. His head swiveled to look up one side of the
street, then down the other. Hooking his thumbs in
the loopholes of his jeans, he began to walk toward
her house with a furious step. His green aviator-style
jacket, the one with the gold star embroidered over
his heart, was hitched up beneath the palms of his

hands. His head, as always, was bare, and his dark hair swirled in the wind.

"Um . . . maybe you should," Cameryn murmured. "He looks pissed."

"Wow. Your very first fight. I want details!" She gave a bounce on the bed. "This is better than trash TV!"

"We are *not* going to fight."

"Wanna bet?"

"Why should we? I've got more security than the president, and it's no big deal. Besides, helping the police is my decision." Cameryn turned to her, defensive, raising her chin and crossing her arms in a way she hoped conveyed confidence. "Andrew said I was being brave."

"That's one word for it." Lyric held up her hands in mock surrender. "Okay, I'll get out of here, since I know when I'm not wanted. Text me later so I can find out what happened. It's so comforting to know I'll be a part of your permanent government file. If I can text you back something creepy, I might do it, just to keep them on their toes."

"Yeah, and you and I can have a nice little visit after they throw your butt in prison."

"Still, it might be kinda fun, messing with the government—"

"Don't even joke around about this stuff. These people are deadly serious. It's the FBI."

"Well, no matter what, I think Justin's going to protect you even better. With him it's personal."

Down below, Cameryn heard the chime of her doorbell followed by the notes of her grandmother's soft Irish lilt. Lyric, in the meantime, wasted no time pulling on her coat. She grabbed her backpack and slung it over her shoulder. Leaning close, she whispered, "Before you guys start yelling I want you both to remember that Valentine's Day is tomorrow—"

"Go!" Cameryn hissed, shoving her friend between her shoulder blades just as she heard her grandmother say, "Yes, Justin, she's in her room."

And then, as she heard her friend and Justin greet each other on the steps, Cameryn smoothed her hair and prepared herself for whatever was about to come.

Chapter Nine

"BEFORE YOU GET your back up, I'm asking that you listen to what I have to say," was the first thing Justin said. "I'm asking that you hear me out until I'm finished before you say no," was the second.

He stopped in the doorway of her room, his lanky body propped against the frame with one leg straight and the other bent. She couldn't tell from the expression on his face whether he was upset, relieved to see her, or some sort of mix in between. One thing was clear—it looked as though Justin meant business.

"Well, hi, Justin," she answered pointedly. "How are you? Me? Oh, I'm fine. I'm a little tired since I was up all night, but thanks for asking."

"Sorry I didn't begin with the usual pleasantries. So how are you?"

"Edgy."

"Don't look so scared, Cammie." He pushed the hair back from his wide-set eyes.

"I'm not," she said. "Just tense. You look tense, too."

"There's a lot to be tense about."

"Yeah." She shrugged. "Lyric's convinced you're going to try to pressure me to get off the case but I told her you wouldn't do that. She thinks we're going to have a fight."

"Shhh." With one hand he held up his finger to his lips and pointed downstairs to where Cameryn's grandmother bustled about. Now that her door was open Cameryn could hear the sound of glasses clinking in the sink and the soft notes of humming.

"Your mammaw can hear every word. I want to talk to you privately. Can we shut your door?"

She shook her head. "Sorry. House rules—no guys allowed in my room with the door closed. My dad's kind of a stickler that way. He's going to be home any minute now. . . ." Again she realized how young her words sounded. Well, she'd be eighteen in a week. Maybe then she could renegotiate.

If Justin minded what she said he didn't let it show. Instead he just smiled his slow smile that made Cameryn guess he actually approved of her father's strictness. "Okay, then can we go anywhere that's a bit more, let's say, confidential?"

Cameryn bit the edge of her lip. "Andrew told me I'm not supposed to leave the premises."

"Then how about that glider?" Justin asked. "I saw your pop left it up. I can brush off the snow and we can talk there. It's still"—he made air quotes—"'on the premises.' And just in case you're still worried about leaving the safety of these four walls . . ." Justin pulled back his jacket to reveal the metal handle of a Glock pistol. "Actually, I hope Kyle comes around. It will make everything a lot easier."

Cameryn looked over at her desk and her computer, deciding. "Okay," she said. "Let me grab my BlackBerry."

Shoving the BlackBerry into the back pocket of her jeans, she followed him, her hand reaching for his as they descended the steps. Justin's palm, always calloused, felt warm in hers, and for a moment she was tempted to let down her guard. But his smile belied a sort of uneasiness—she could sense it in him. Well, he could do his worst and she wouldn't change her mind. Long ago she'd learned to stand up for herself and she wasn't about to change now.

"I've got to get my coat," she said. "It's in the closet. You get to tell Mammaw we're going outside."

"Oh, so you want me to break the news so that *I* can take the bullet."

"Yep." Cameryn grinned. "Don't worry, you've already

charmed her. She's baking again—Valentine sugar cookies. Try to snag us a couple if you can."

The closet was bursting with coats of all shapes and sizes. Cameryn was glad Justin couldn't see how unorganized the Mahoneys really were, at least when it came to their undersized closets. Her grandmother's coat made from lamb's wool jammed up against her father's heavy parkas and down vests, which were in turn compressed against Cameryn's snowboarding pants and summer jackets. Snow boots had been placed in a line, one next to the other, in a formation so tight they looked like bowling pins. She found her tan and brown pair from L.L. Bean and tugged them on, then slipped into her coat, pausing just long enough to catch a glimpse of herself in the entryway mirror.

Oh, great, she said to herself. Her hair was impossible, mostly because she'd given it only a cursory brushing that morning and now it sprung from her head like tree roots. It wasn't just her hair that was out of control. Her skin was pale, and dark smudges shadowed the area beneath her eyes. She looked . . . haunted. For a fleeting moment she thought of pinching her cheeks, a fast way, her grandmother once told her, to "bring back the roses," but decided against it.

A small shelf beneath the mirror contained knick-knacks. Among the various keys and paper clips she found a cinnamon ChapStick, an elastic, and a peppermint wrapped in cellophane. As fast as she could, Cameryn pulled up her hair and yanked it through the elastic at the base of her neck, applied a thin coat of ChapStick, and popped the mint into her mouth. Well, it was something, she told herself, and the best she could do.

"Hey, are you coming, Cammie?" Justin called from the kitchen.

"Yeah," she said, zipping her coat to her chin and digging her gloves from the pockets. She, at least, was aware of how cold February air could get high in the mountains. When she stepped into their kitchen she drank in the vanilla smell. Her grandmother was squeezing a pastry bag filled with red frosting.

"These look like they were made in a bakery."

Mammaw, who had a smudge of flour on her face, glanced up at Justin and smiled like a schoolgirl. "There're just cookies, plain and simple. Off with you now," she said, shooing both of them through the door. "And don't stay out too long, it's about to get dark. A hat, Cammie," her grandmother called out after them, a dictum Cameryn chose not to hear. She looked at the large thermometer that had been nailed to the outside wall of their house. The temperature read seventeen degrees.

"Your mammaw really gets into the holidays," Justin said, gingerly holding two heart-shaped cookies on a napkin balanced on the palm of his hand. The paving stones that led to the glider were buried beneath a layer of snow, but her father had shoveled a path that led to the back of the house. The snow on either side of them was three feet high, so they had to walk single file. Justin led the way.

"Unfortunately, we have decorations for *every* occasion. You should see what she does for St. Patrick's Day—green pancakes, green beer. Personally, I think the whole 'holiday cheer' thing can get a bit cheesy."

"We had too many kids in my family for my mom to have time to decorate or bake or do any of that kind of thing. Everything came from a box. For a while there I thought Sara Lee was my aunt."

"Well, I can't cook, so don't get your hopes up. The cooking gene is one I did *not* inherit. No baking, no nothing. Nada."

"I'm a big boy. I know how to open a can."

They stopped in front of the glider. Behind it, a clutch of aspen stretched out bare arms, their tissuelike bark studded with knotholes. "By the way," Cameryn said, suddenly serious, "am I being watched? Right now, I mean."

"Yeah," Justin nodded. "They're out there."

"I guess I'm glad. I mean, I want to be safe. But it feels kind of . . . weird. I hate being spied on. I'll be so happy when this is all over."

"That's actually what I wanted to talk to you about." His tone had shifted and there was something new in his voice that made her nervous. He cocked his head as he looked down at her, his eyes narrowing. She could tell he was searching for the right words for what he'd come to say. "Maybe we should sit," he suggested. With his bare hand Justin began to brush off the glider, still carefully holding the cookies in the other.

"I've got gloves on—let me do that. I'm not helpless," Cameryn told him as she scooped an armful of powder onto the cement below.

"No. You're not." She heard it again, the flint in his voice.

"So what's the big secret that you're sure I'll say no to?" she asked, facing him once more. His thick-heeled boots made him even taller so that he loomed above her. His eyes had darkened to the color of water before a storm. He hesitated.

"Justin—what is it?"

"All right, I'll just say it. I don't want you to be a part of the investigation." He set the cookies on the edge of the glider, then placed a hand on each of her shoulders. "It's not safe for you and I think—no, I'm *sure*—it's wrong for you to be involved. I know you're doing this because Kyle threatened me, but he can't hurt me. Look, I'm asking you to drop the case. I'm asking you to drop it for me."

She raised her chin just a little, making sure her eyes stayed locked on his. Well, she'd guessed this was coming. "Tempting, but no," she said.

"Cammie! Just listen for once. You don't understand—"

"I *do* understand and the answer is no. *No!*"

"But you can't say no before you hear me out."

"I just did. No, no, and no."

"Talking with Kyle, egging him on in any way—it's just dangerous." There was a new heat to his voice, but Cameryn shook her head with every word he spoke.

"My dad says I can do it. Andrew thinks I can help—"

"Your father is a coroner, not a lawman, and the agent's main concern is catching Kyle, not protecting you. My number one priority is keeping you safe. There's a difference." He squeezed her shoulders but she pulled away. A thousand feelings were crowding inside her and she wasn't sure she could sort them all out, not with him looking at her the way he was, guilty and sure of himself all at once.

Justin rubbed the back of his neck. "You want to keep me safe and I want to keep you safe. We're both stubborn, aren't we?"

"Yes."

"I guess there's a lot we need to learn about each other. Here's something you should know about me:

I will do whatever it takes. So you might as well hear the worst of it."

"There's more?" She crossed her arms over her chest and took a step back. She did not like this conversation. "What did you do?"

He seemed to waver a moment. "I went to Durango and talked to Dr. Moore." A breath, and then he exhaled slowly, creating a frosty plume. "I told him what was going on and . . . I asked him to help me talk you out of this crazy scheme."

Cameryn stared at him, for a moment too stunned to speak. Finally, she managed to ask, "Why?"

"Because you respect the guy and I figured he's the only one you might listen to. You're still a minor, Cammie, even if it's just for a few days. The feds should not have asked you to do this. The doc understands exactly who these FBI goons are asking you to play with and how high the stakes are—"

"You did *what*?" There was a feeling rising above the rest. It was anger. It shot up her spine and exploded in her head and she could feel her nostrils flare as she cried, "How could you—Dr. Moore is my mentor and—you, what did you say, that I'm just some little kid who couldn't handle it? He's going to think . . . you had no right, Justin!" Her words tumbled out of her mouth before she could line them up properly so that they made sense. But even though her thoughts were fragmented, Justin seemed to be able to follow her intent well enough.

"Calm down, Cammie!"

"I *hate* it when people tell me to calm down. Since we're learning new things about each other you ought to know that. And by the way, if I'm old enough for you to date, I'm certainly old enough to make my own decisions. *Why* did you talk to Dr. Moore?"

"I already told you."

She almost stomped her foot. "That is so bloody patronizing. This is my decision, not yours."

"I thought it could be *ours*!" he said, matching her heat. "This is what *I* do. Could you give me just a little credit here? I understand the law. I know the criminal mind. And I'm asking you to respect that and walk away from this case. Cameryn, don't let Kyle's threat against me get into your head. He can't hurt me but he *can* hurt you. I'm asking you to do this one thing for me." He was pleading now.

"I already told you. No."

"Cammie, come *on*!"

She swore under her breath and turned away, but his hand was on her arm and he pulled her around to face him again. He seemed to be straining to keep his voice even. She had never seen him angry like this, at least not with anger directed her way. Or was it fear? She couldn't tell and she didn't care. A gust of wind blew against her back, causing the bare twigs of aspen to shiver overhead. The wind wound its way up Justin's arms and into his hair, lifting the locks gently before setting them down again, and beyond that she saw a spray of ice crystals that blew over the cookies, blotting out the pink frosting her mammaw had carefully written in scroll.

"For the record, Dr. Moore agreed with me. He thinks the FBI is way out of line."

"Oh, so you got him on your side. Good for you." Her heart was pumping so hard she didn't feel the need for her coat. One single idea beat through her: just because he'd kissed her, Justin Crowley thought he was entitled to run her life. Did he really think that four years' seniority allowed him to make choices for her? Was that what her grandmother had tried to warn her about—that the one who was older had more power? So, he got Dr. Moore on his side. Checkmate. Only what Justin failed to understand was he'd just lost the game.

"Stop staring at me and say something," Justin demanded.

"I have one question. Did you screw things up between me and Dr. Moore?"

He looked confused. "What are you talking about?"

"Stop. Just . . . stop." She peeled his hand from her elbow and took a step back. She could not believe how cold she sounded. "Dr. Moore asked me to come to Durango and look over the Safer case. Does he still want me to help him, or did you convince him I'm just a 'minor' who can't even think?"

"One thing doesn't have anything to do with the other."

"Just answer my question. Please."

"Fine." His voice had turned as cold as the air. "Dr. Moore still wants you to come down tomorrow, if that's what you're asking."

"That's what I'm asking. You screwed me over to make a point. I don't like people going behind my back, Justin." She was mad enough that the next words came out of her mouth before she had time to think them through. "For me that's a deal breaker."

Justin's eyes flashed. "Don't you think you're being just a little bit melodramatic? Using words like *deal breaker* when we've just barely gotten started."

Raising her chin, she said, "You should never have involved Dr. Moore. Stay out of my business."

Justin jerked his fingers through his hair and spun to the side. He jammed his hands into his pockets. "Okay. You won't listen to me because at seventeen you have all the answers. You know what? Maybe you *are* too young."

The wind had polished the top crust of snow so that it looked crystalline, as though diamond powder had been tossed across, pale blue in the waning light. Were the police out there, listening? Well, if they were, she didn't care, because there was nothing more to say.

Maybe you are *too young.*

Each word was a slap. He'd pushed her and she'd pushed back hard, and now their words were out there, curling up in the winter air like smoke. She waited for him to take it back but he just looked at her with an expression she couldn't read, and then she could feel tears threatening to spill into her eyes. There was no way she would let him see those. Without another word she turned, threading her way back down the shoveled path. She heard Justin follow her, his boots scuffing, his breath coming in short bursts, and then he walked past her. There was the slam of his car door and a muted squeal as his tires spun out against the snow.

Swallowing back her emotion, she opened the back door. The inside warmth seemed strangely oppressive.

"Cammie, what has happened?" her mammaw cried, brushing her hands against her Valentine apron.

"Nothing," Cameryn answered, hurrying by. Mammaw, reading Cameryn's expression, knew enough to leave her alone.

She jerked off her coat. How had it all gone so wrong? She had overreacted; she had always had a temper that she tried to keep under wraps, but this time it had all bubbled up, and now she'd made a mess of things. And yet, Justin had been wrong, too. His male ego made him think Kyle couldn't touch him, but she knew better. She'd weighed the risks and made a decision and Justin didn't honor it. Wiping the tears from her cheeks, Cameryn threw her boots into the closet. Her BlackBerry hummed in her pocket and she rubbed her face with the palm of her hand. Was it Justin calling to apologize? Or worse.

The number, though, was one she recognized. It belonged to Dr. Moore.

"Hello?" she said. Clearing her throat, she tried to take the waver out. "Dr. Moore?"

"Hello, Miss Mahoney," Dr. Moore said. "I trust things are going well for you?"

"I'm okay," she said. "Is something wrong?"

"Yes. You remember I asked you to come down tomorrow? I'm afraid there's been a change in plans."

Cameryn's heart fell. So, Justin had ruined it for her, after all. But before she could begin to form her argument, Dr. Moore said, "If you're up for it, I'd like you to come down right now. I wouldn't ask but it's important."

"Is this about Brent Safer and Joseph Stein? About the jelly in the lungs?"

"Yes, and no. There is something I need you to see."

"I—I don't understand," Cameryn stammered.

"I don't want to say more over the phone," he said, and she immediately understood he was being vague for the benefit of the police. "But let me say this: the case just got a lot bigger."

"What do you mean?"

"I mean the game has changed."

It took her a moment to form the words. "What's this about?"

"You. I'll expect you and your father within the hour."

Chapter Ten

"CAMMIE, HONEY, IT'S time to wake up. We're here."

"What?" Cameryn struggled to sit up from the front seat of the station wagon. "Dad, why did you let me sleep?"

"It's good for you—you were up all night."

"But—what time is it?"

"Five thirty. I have to admit I'm feeling robbed. I was fully prepared for a father-daughter chat, but you were so quiet at first I thought I should leave you be. Then I realized you were out. Well, sleep's the best thing, anyway."

She remembered only a little—the trees whizzing by, dark green against the snow, until it had all blurred as she'd given in to sleep. "Yeah, well, I seem to be zoning out a lot lately. Sorry." Stretching her arms over her head as far as she could, Cameryn quickly realized they were already stopped outside the plain red brick Medical Examiner's Building. The station wagon's engine clacked and wheezed as they waited in front of the metal garage door. The building's flat roof supported a thick layer of snow. Icicles hung off the gutter in a row that looked like jagged glass. Her father tapped the horn, a signal for Ben to open up.

The side of her cheek felt numb and there was a kink in her neck. As she shook off the grogginess of sleep she felt the sensation of her heart dropping through her, resting like a stone in the bottom of her belly. Justin. The fight.

Her father tapped the horn again and a moment later the door began to roll into the ceiling, revealing Ben's legs dressed in blood-splattered green scrubs. He waved them in.

"Man, your engine sounds bad," Ben said as Cameryn and her father got out of the station wagon. "You better get your hearse in for a tune-up."

"I know, I know, it's just that it's getting harder and harder to find parts for a car this old." Patrick patted the car's hood fondly. "But it just keeps on going. And you can't fit a body into any old car—these station wagons were almost made for the job. So where are we heading, Ben, to the office or the morgue?"

Ben looked uncomfortable. His hand tugged at his collar as he said, "Well, here's the thing. You know how I do all the dirty work around here? Moore asked me to ask you if it's okay if he talks to your girl all by himself— just for a minute. He wants her to go to his office."

Her father looked stunned. "Why would he want to do that? I'm the coroner."

Ben shrugged. "Moore says it's a personal matter between him and Cammie. Hey, don't shoot me, I'm only the messenger."

She could tell that her father was about to say no. Leaning back on his heels, he hooked his thumbs into his jacket pockets and frowned, but Ben said in his pleasing, mellow voice, "Dr. Moore wants you and me to go on to Histology. It's just for a little while."

Cameryn tried to tamp down the irritation that surged inside her. It was happening all over again. Other people, male people, were talking about her and making decisions for her. "I'll go talk to Dr. Moore," she said to her father. Then she turned to Ben. "By the way, I'm old enough to answer for myself. Eighteen in just a few days, remember? I'll meet up with you guys in Histology."

Her words seemed to balloon out into the very corners of the garage. Ben looked nervously from Cameryn to Patrick, then back again. Finally, her father said, "I guess it's been decided."

"All right then, Miss Almost-Legal," Ben answered, looking relieved. "You know the way, right?"

"First door past the autopsy suite."

She could feel their eyes on her as she walked up the concrete ramp. They didn't follow right away. As she opened the door she stole a quick glimpse and saw her father's hands moving through the air, although he spoke so softly she couldn't make out the words. Ben merely shook his head from side to side.

Down the hallways she went, stopping only briefly to let Amber know she was there to see Dr. Moore. Eyeing her up and down, Amber waved Cameryn through, and soon Cameryn found herself knocking on a gray metal door that had a plastic nameplate stamped DR. JOSEPH MOORE, FORENSIC PATHOLOGIST.

"Come in."

The door creaked on its hinges as Cameryn stepped inside. "You asked to see me, Dr. Moore?"

"I did. Sit down, Miss Mahoney," he said, and motioned her to a brown chair with metal legs. "And shut the door."

His office was small, claustrophobically so. Dr. Moore sat hunched at his desk poring over an open file, his reading glasses resting on the tip of his bulbous nose. "One moment," he said as his finger glided down the page.

"Sure. Take your time."

He nodded and continued reading. The desk was buried beneath neatly stacked folders whose pages bristled with multicolored tabs. Two bookshelves took up what little floor space was left, and three more were bracketed to the walls. Each was filled with medical books and forensic journals, arranged according to height. One solitary shelf had been dedicated to plastic models of various organs: a red- and blue-veined heart sat next to a plastic eye with a removable lens.

Directly to her right hung a painting of a meadow that looked different from the cheap art that lined the hallway walls. In this painting, grasses bent beneath an unseen wind while flowers nodded on the ends of long stalks. But the flowers weren't the star of the scene. Colors in the painting consisted mainly of various hues of green mixed with yellows and browns. In extremely small, unobtrusive letters she made out the name *Moore* etched in the bottom corner.

He shut the folder and looked up at her, his hands folding together so that his fingers intertwined.

"This is yours?" she asked.

"Yes. I like to paint. But I've always seen things differently than most. My wife prodded me to put flowers in my meadow, but I personally like the grasses. The grasses and the leaves are what I find beautiful."

"The leaves?"

"Yes. In my opinion the buds get all the glory, but

it's the leaves that keep the plant alive. Rather like forensics. The surgeons on high are the roses of the medical world, but we who choose forensics make the bloom possible. Sit," he said again, and this time she sank into the brown chair.

"I'm not sure I understand . . ."

"It doesn't matter. Just the musings of an old man. We have other things to discuss today." He took off his glasses and pinched the bridge of his nose. She'd never seen him without his glasses before. The skin around his eyes was riddled with fine wrinkles, like the cracks in a Ming vase. He was minus his white lab coat, another first. His cotton shirt was a blue checkered pattern that he'd buttoned up almost to his collar, which was crisp with starch. "Well, Miss Mahoney, here you are. And here I am. And I don't quite know where to begin."

This, too, was odd. Dr. Moore, so caustic and abrupt, had always charged forth, never at a loss for words or purpose. Cameryn tried to swallow back the nervousness she was beginning to feel. She unzipped her parka and hung it on the back of the chair carefully, making sure it was centered. "You said the case involved me. The Safer case," she prompted.

"Yes. But before I get into the technicalities I feel I should give you a reason. One thing builds upon the other, you see. I need you to . . . understand . . . why

I'm prepared to breach ethics. I've never done that, not in forty-one years in this macabre business. But I'm ready to do it now."

She felt her eyes go wide. Something was definitely wrong. "Dr. Moore—"

"I see a bit of myself in you, Miss Mahoney. The same fire, the same passion, your willingness to fight." He picked up the file he'd been reading, then inexplicably set it down. "Do you remember that first day when I met you?" He wasn't talking to her, exactly. His words seemed to be aimed at the file. "I'm afraid I was a bit hard on you then. But your father said you had a gift, a gift for forensics. Patrick was right and I was wrong."

"You've taught me a lot, Dr. Moore."

"Have I? I'd like to think what we do is important."

"If it weren't for people like you and me then the dead would die without any kind of voice. You're the one who told me that."

"Precisely." He nodded and looked at her with unwavering eyes. "All this time I've worked with death, around death, through death, I've never stopped to think about the thing itself. The fact of the matter is . . ." His voiced trailed off.

"What is it, Dr. Moore?"

Dr. Moore's jowly head bowed and his eyebrows rose as he said in a flat, emotionless voice, "I have cancer,

Miss Mahoney. So death has finally and inevitably come knocking, but this time it's on my own door."

Cameryn sat frozen while *cancer* spiraled through the air as if it were a nebula. She breathed the word in and exhaled it and the word kept unwinding into the corners of the room. "What kind?" she asked softly.

"Renal cell carcinoma. Kidney. It's in my left kidney." He sounded as though he were recounting statistics on a report. "I've not shared this yet with my staff so I'm asking you to keep this in confidence. Will you?"

"Yes." She paused. "How bad is it?"

"Clinically, my doctor hopes it's contained to stage two. Pathologically, well, I'll have the final answer after my surgery, which is scheduled for next week. So you see, time has become a priority for me."

"I'm—I'm so sorry."

"Well, so am I, but there it is. I'm not dead yet," he said, with a bit of his old bite. "However, what I said about time didn't concern me. It concerns you." He pushed the file to the edge of the desk and this time Cameryn could see his fingers tremble every so slightly. "Your young man came here and asked me to convince you to drop your involvement in the Kyle O'Neil case."

This again. Cameryn looked down at the carpet, shabby and brown. There was a frayed patch the chair wheels had worn thin.

"Deputy Crowley is quite right to be concerned."

"I can handle it."

"Can you?" He smiled tolerantly. "You do understand that O'Neil is a psychopath." He said this in a way that was neither a statement nor a question.

"Yes. I know. Sheriff Jacobs told me that a long time ago."

"Perhaps you don't understand what that entails. A colleague of mine in Arizona has conducted research on the psychopathic mind. He believes there may be an actual physical component to the disorder, although it's too soon to be sure. The amygdala—that's the emotional hub of the brain—may play a part. Or perhaps a disruption to the paralimbic region of the brain."

She looked at him blankly. She couldn't seem to keep her mind on the conversation, because the thoughts of cancer and her mentor's death drowned out the rest of his words rushing past her in a verbal wave. Instead, she had a memory. Of Dr. Moore, his eyes alight, explaining the words he'd painted on the autopsy room wall in his own delicate hand. *Hic locus est ubi mors gaudet succurrere vitae.* This is the place where death delights to help the living. He'd taken so much joy in teaching her, in giving to her, in saving her. Other than helping with a few forensic cases, she'd never really done much for Dr. Moore, and that made her sad.

". . . makes all the difference. Are you listening?"

"I'm sorry . . . the what?"

"Miss Mahoney, I am trying to get you to understand. A psychopath does not feel what we feel. In extreme cases, such as O'Neil's, the person is crafty and manipulative and utterly without conscience. They are among the most dangerous of people who walk our planet. I want you to look at his handiwork." He placed the manila file into her hands.

She looked from him to the folder and back again. "Is this the Safer file?"

"No. It's not." For a moment his fingers lingered until he slowly pulled them away. He picked up his glasses and put them on, and once again his eyes seemed overlarge for his face. Rolling his chair so close his knees touched hers, he said, "This is the file of Ed Staskiewicz. Leather Ed, I believe you called him. Open it."

Hadn't everyone already told her that to become a part of Leather Ed's case would be an ethical violation? And yet here he was, handing her documents that were clearly off-limits, and she felt a new anxiety overtake her. She looked away, into the painting that had a meadow filled with grasses. That was where she wished she could be, wandering along the stalks where the steel gray of the sky met the golden tops of wheat, away from this office and away from death.

"You think me unethical."

"No. No, I'm just . . . confused."

"This is something you *must* see." With surprising gravity, Moore said, "Yesterday I would have stood my ground and followed the rules of the system. But my illness has caused me to question certain . . . things. The bigger picture, you could say." His eyes were examining her closely. "Look at the manner of death, Miss Mahoney. Try to understand the danger."

Tentatively, Cameryn pulled back the manila cover. The first thing she saw were pictures of Leather Ed, still propped in the chair, recorded in color and black-and-white and snapped from every angle. She had hardly taken the time to look at him when she discovered his body in the room, but now she could examine him more closely. The fingertips had been chewed off, revealing stubs of white bone, and the lower portion of Leather Ed's face was gone. His bottom row of teeth looked like the keys on a piano. His leather pants, taut from decomposition, had holes along the seams, and the shirt was taut across the middle.

Cameryn's eyes scanned the table where she'd found the note and she could see the outline where the note had been because the rest of the wood lay shrouded in a thin layer of dust. Next to that imprint were two plants. One had silver-green leaves while the other sported pale orange blossoms shooting from a bract—strange notes of life that flowered next to death.

Dr. Moore tapped his knuckles against the picture. "It's the report, not the photographs, that I want you to examine."

Obediently, Cameryn leafed through the rest of the materials, charts inscribed in Dr. Moore's precise hand, as well as a sheet of paper with the weight of the organs written to the side in blue ink and carefully recorded in neat columns, with the standard outline of a man's body that had been illustrated to reflect each injury. At the back, she found a copy of the death certificate, then the autopsy report.

"Do you see it?" Dr. Moore pointed with his index finger. Next to the words *Cause of Death* was listed *Asphyxia due to unknown substance.*

A sudden understanding flashed through her mind. "Are you saying—"

"I am. Leather Ed died from the same substance in his lungs that killed Stein and Safer."

"But—how could Kyle get to three different men?" In a timid, breaking voice, she said, "Those other two guys were from Hollywood. Leather Ed was a recluse. Stein and Safer died in Durango, Leather Ed in Silverton. What is the connection?"

"I don't know. But I'm not asking you to solve this, I'm asking you to consider the danger you are in. Leather Ed died in the exact same manner as Stein and Safer. The alveoli were clogged with the identical gel. O'Neil killed *all* of them. He may have killed more. A high school girl, no matter how bright, should stay away."

Cameryn could feel it, the cracks in her composure. Fear stabbed through her. Tears welled in her eyes but she made herself blink them back until she could get her thoughts righted once again. This was no time to give in to panic. It would be exactly what Kyle would want her to do.

"I'm not trying to be a sensationalist." Dr. Moore took her hands into his own. "But Cameryn, you cannot dance with the devil. Kyle O'Neil is without conscience. He kills in cold blood. I'm asking you to step away from all of this."

"I will."

Dr. Moore's brow had been furrowed but now light appeared in his eyes in rays of relief. He reached over and patted Cameryn's arm. "I'm glad you're listening to reason. I've seen the headstrong side of you so long that I assumed I'd be in for a battle."

"I will walk away," she answered calmly, "as soon as Kyle O'Neil is locked up in prison. I want to read the rest of this file and then I'd like you to take me to see Leather Ed. Is his body still here?"

Confused, Dr. Moore answered, "Yes, he's in the cooler. But—"

Cameryn shook her head. "I've got a quick call to

make and then I need to go through these files. Kyle typed a message to me, Dr. Moore. He said 'you can see my mind in what I left behind.' There is something in here, in these files or on that body, that he left for me. This is about *me*."

"That is not why I brought you here." Dr. Moore's face darkened. "The threat—"

"It doesn't matter." She almost laughed at the absurdity of the idea of safety. "I'll be in danger until he is caught. Life is risky, Dr. Moore. I could get sick or get struck by a car. The truth is there is no place to hide. No one is ever really safe."

"But to be so incautious when the stakes are life and death—"

"That's just it," Cameryn interrupted. "I don't want to be cautious. I don't want to be a victim anymore. Look, you're right, I *am* a fighter. You fight your battle and you can watch me fight mine. And I can guarantee you something." Now it was she who reached out to squeeze Dr. Moore's gnarled hands.

His voice turned suddenly husky as he asked, "What could you possibly guarantee?"

"We're going to win." She pressed her thumb across the back of his hand. "Both of us. Cancer, crazy people, whatever, bring it on. Just watch what we can do."

Chapter Eleven

DR. MOORE EMERGED from his office with Leather Ed's file clutched in his hand. His lab coat hung loose-ly at his sides. He watching her, eagle-eyed, as she quickly snapped her BlackBerry shut. Her *'Bye* hung in the air.

"I gave you a moment of privacy, just as you asked," he said. "So tell me, Miss Mahoney, whom did you call?"

She shook her head.

"You aren't going to tell me?" His eyebrows rose up into his forehead, causing the skin to pleat.

Cameryn, who had been leaning against the wall, hopped forward. "Not yet. I want to see how it plays out. I left a message."

"So you're saying you prefer to remain mysterious." The deep grooves on either side of his mouth reached all the way down to his jawbone, which gave the impression of a perpetual frown. "After your little pep talk I thought we were on the same team. No matter." He waved her protests away. "You asked to see the remains of Leather Ed. Against my better judgment, I'm prepared to comply. But make no mistake; I will keep you on a tight leash. Shall we?" He swept his hand toward the hallway and she understood the unspoken message immediately. Whatever vulnerability he'd shared with her was to be kept private, and he wanted no dramatics as they stepped back into the real world. He was once again the commander of his ship. And yet . . . something had changed. She could see it in his eyes. A single emotional thread stretched between Dr. Moore and Cameryn, a sentimental filament that bound them, one to another. He cared about her, no matter what his gruff exterior showed.

"Follow me, Miss Mahoney," he said with a brisk nod. Walking at a hurried pace he escorted Cameryn through the autopsy suite, flipping on a bank of lights. It was the first time she'd seen it empty. Ben, she guessed, must be in the histology lab with her father, and it surprised her to see how still the place looked, like a carnival where all the rides had shut down. The cavernous sinks were empty, the gurneys were gone, the floor had been mopped clean, all the tools whisked away and countertops laid bare. Dr. Moore's shoes squeaked against the tile as he walked, while Cameryn heard her own staccato rhythm, amplified because she wore no booties to muffle the sound.

"Have you been in the cooler?" the doctor asked.

"Yes. Once."

He pivoted on one foot and began walking backwards, as graceful as a dancer. "You may want to reconsider going in there. Do you remember the decedent was in full decomp?"

"I remember," she said, shuddering at the memory.

"Yes, well, the dog, of course, damaged the facial tissue and outer extremities. It was the lungs that told the story. I don't know what you expect to find on his remains."

"I'm not sure, either," Cameryn replied. "When is he going to be released to a funeral home?"

"I have no idea. So far we've got no next of kin." With impeccable timing, Dr. Moore spun forward again and placed his palm against the handle of the door. "And here we are."

Moore pulled on the metal lever and ushered her inside. Cold air, heavy with the stench, hit her full in the face, and she tried for a moment to hold her breath. Cupping her hand over her nose she walked on, her eyes filming as the smell rolled over her. Dr. Moore flipped on the lights, which came on one row at a time, like those in a stadium.

She tried not to register the bodies resting on shelves like packages of meat in a deli. There were seven of them in total. Six decedents rested on stainless steel shelves stacked against the wall, but the seventh and farthest away still lay on a metal gurney. White cotton sheets had been placed over each body, including the head, but the feet remained exposed. Each decedent wore a toe tag. She followed Dr. Moore past a body whose toenails were painted a seashell pink. Another set of feet belonged to a man whose nails were as thick as a rhino's hide.

"Are Safer and Stein here?" she whispered. Clearing her throat she repeated the question, louder this time. There was no need to speak softly when everyone who might listen in on her conversation was dead.

"No, they're long gone. Their publicists couldn't get them out fast enough. Vultures." Dr. Moore spat the word. "I've been holding off the media by telling them the tests results haven't come in yet, but my phone hasn't stopped ringing—everybody wants to score the juicy details. I despise celebrity deaths."

"People go wild when someone famous dies, but no one cares about Leather Ed. But life is still . . . life," she said.

"Oh, I remember the heady days of youth, when I was an idealist, too," Dr. Moore answered her. "I've learned through the years that life is not fair. He's at the end, the one on the autopsy tray."

The refrigerator hum was loud in her ears. The body

at the farthest end had toes that had turned a purplish black. The tag read *Edward Staskiewicz*.

Reflexively, Cameryn clamped her hand tighter over her nose, but it was no use. The stench penetrated her fingers and she breathed him in, the odor thick enough to taste. Dr. Moore, though, seemed unfazed as he stepped to the right of Leather Ed's head. With an expert motion he rolled back the sheet all the way to just above Leather Ed's groin. "He came in with boots on and Ben had a devil of a time getting them off. In the end he had to slice them with a carpet knife. We had to cut off his leathers, too. My guess is he had been dead for three weeks, although I'm sure the cool air slowed his decomposition. As you know, declaring time of death is never an exact science."

"Uh-huh. Especially when the body is in putrefaction." Cameryn forced her thoughts to turn away from the smell and concentrate instead on what remained. This was what told the story. *She could see his mind in what he left behind.* Something told her the answer was there for the taking, if only she could see it. She leaned closer, the clinical side of her mind firing up as she studied the coiled gray hair that rested like metal filings against the tray. She took in the long lobes of his ears and the white hair matted thick on his chest, the huge stitches that reached to his navel, the paper white look of his skin. Livor mortis had settled into his hip area, which made the flesh appear a deep rose. His abdomen, though, had turned a mossy green, and green streaks that formed along the veins snaked up into his shoulders and chest.

"That greenish color comes from what we called marbleization," Dr. Moore explained. "Ben calls it 'Shrek green.' You see the blisters along his skin?"

Cameryn nodded.

"Those contain serous fluid. It's all part of the fermentation process. His leather clothes kept him together, which, in its way, was helpful. Fortunately he did not enter the black stage of putrefaction. In the black stage the body cavity actually ruptures. Tomorrow we'll put him into the freezer."

If he was testing her to see if she would fold, it did no good. She forced herself to lower her hand from her mouth. "Can I see his legs?"

"Be my guest." Grabbing the sheet from the ankles, he pulled it up. Cameryn peered at Leather Ed's shins, then his feet. There was mottling here, with white circles that looked like popcorn against deep purple, green, and blue, but there was nothing unusual. His hair was finer around his ankles, sparse. Concentrating hard, she began at the head and worked her way to the feet, then back to the head again, bending close to examine the bones of his fingers, pulling back to get an overview of his remains. What was she missing?

Kyle was egging her on, she knew it. He'd left pieces for her. He wanted her to find something. But what?

"You want me to roll him over, or will the photographs suffice?" Dr. Moore asked, tapping the file against his thigh. "I can tell you there's nothing on his back except more livor and some skin slippage. What's your pleasure?"

"The photographs will be fine," she said, disappointed that she'd found nothing, but eager to get away from the odor. "Let's go."

With an expert motion, Dr. Moore unfurled the sheet so that it settled down against Leather Ed, adjusting it at the head and tugging it around his feet. Cameryn marveled that the doctor didn't wear gloves. There was no way she wanted to touch what remained of that body with her own bare skin.

"I suggest we adjourn to the histology lab. I'd like to show you microscopic pieces of his lung, and then show you lung samples from Safer and Stein. Perhaps we could go to Toxicology and see if the results are complete. Really, Miss Mahoney, there's nothing here."

"Where are his clothes? And the book he was holding? I'd like to get a look at that book."

Dr. Moore escorted her back into the autopsy suite, saying, "I've got everything bagged in the cooler, but they won't stay here. Since Silverton's too small to have refrigerated storage, the items will be sent out to CBI tomorrow. That evidence is not my concern. A medical examiner looks only to the body. As to the rest, well, I'm afraid that's not my department."

"You're right," said a voice. "It's mine."

Cameryn's heart leapt when she saw Justin's tall, lanky frame standing by the large metal sinks. His face looked wary, as though he wasn't sure what to expect from her.

"You came!" she cried. "I wasn't sure you would when I left you that message. How did you get here so fast?"

"Because I've been tailing you. I'm the law, remember?" His lips curled more on one side in the way that she loved. "Listen, Cammie, I know we didn't leave on the best of terms, and that was my fault. But even if you hate me I'm going to keep you safe."

"Don't be stupid. I don't hate you."

"Well, that's something, anyway." His eyes shifted to Dr. Moore. "So, was your luck any better than mine? Did you convince her?"

"I'm sorry, Deputy. She's a very obstinate girl. Woman," Moore added, correcting himself.

"Yeah," Justin said, "there's a lot of that going around. Stubbornness, I mean."

There was a pause. The large clock on the wall made little clicking sounds, louder than Cameryn would ever have imagined. Words that she wanted to say were jammed up in her throat, and Dr. Moore was still there, a silent witness.

Crossing his arms over his chest, Dr. Moore directed his words to Justin. "I called Sheriff Jacobs earlier today. Did the sheriff tell you what I found in Leather Ed's lungs?"

"I got the memo. O'Neil killed them all. Why do you think I followed Cameryn down here?"

Moore nodded, satisfied. "You should know that I showed Miss Mahoney everything. In the end I felt it . . . important . . . for her to understand O'Neil's mind. It goes against protocol, but there it is."

"I'm glad you did." Justin was saying the words to Dr. Moore but all the while looking at Cameryn. "I think I've underestimated her. Maybe we all have."

Her throat tightened, but she forced herself to get the words out. "The minute I found out, the person I wanted to call was you."

"Really?"

"Really."

He was looking at her, low-lidded, and neither one of them said a word. Dr. Moore shifted uncomfortably. "Well, I am getting a sense that I should leave you two alone." He cleared his throat as he stood waiting for one of them to say something in reply, but the pause turned awkward when neither she nor Justin corrected him; Dr. Moore was right, Cameryn did want him to leave. She stayed where she was, rooted to the floor, her nerves on high alert as she looked into Justin's bottomless eyes. Justin stared back from twenty feet away.

"Okay, then." Dr. Moore set the file on one of the desks. "Here is the information you left me, Deputy. I'll be in the histology lab. I trust you two won't be long."

"Not too long," Justin said. He never took his eyes off of Cameryn as Dr. Moore moved quietly out the door. She could hear it click behind him and after that only her breathing. Energy buzzed inside her, heating her skin, but she stood frozen. Justin was the one who moved first. He began to walk toward her, closing the gap, and she found herself moving as well. "Justin, I'm sorry," she said, her words coming in fits and starts. "I know I've got a temper. I guess it's the Irish in me and I really shouldn't have—"

"No, I'm the one," he said, cutting her off. "I should never have tried to convince you like that. You're right. And you're old enough—I should never have said that—"

"Believe it or not, now I'm glad you talked to Dr. Moore—"

"You are?"

"Yes!"

"Then I'm forgiven." His eyes grew soft in appeal. "I *am* forgiven, aren't I?"

"Am *I*?" she asked.

She stopped, only inches away from him now. They were smiling at each other, and she noticed once again that he had beautiful teeth, white as pearls in his suntanned face. He took her hands and pressed his thumbs into her palms. "What would you think if I kissed you in the middle of a morgue?"

"It sounds kind of twisted. And kind of good."

"That's exactly what I thought." He leaned in closer, but Cameryn pulled back, amazed. "You know what? Lyric was right. We had our very first fight."

"It wasn't so bad. And you know what they say about making up." His grin was faunlike, his eyebrows arched. And then he was kissing her, and she didn't think of all the people who had been dissected in this room or of the instruments, shiny and sharp, that were tucked away behind cupboard doors. This was a place where people's insides were revealed. It was almost poetic that in this unlikeliest of spaces she had opened herself to him, not just physically, but by giving him a bit of her soul. She could feel it, the letting go as she kissed him back. Life in the place of death, made sweeter still because this feeling had withstood the heat of angry words.

Draping her arms around his neck, she stood on the tips of her toes, pushing into him hard, kissing him in a way she didn't know she could. For a moment he broke free, surprised and, she could tell, pleased.

"Wow," he said. Cupping her face in his hands, he rested his forehead against hers. "I'll never say you're too young again." His voice was husky, low. "If I'd known this would happen I would have bossed you around sooner."

"Don't even think about it!"

"Man, this making-up thing is good." His lips pressed into hers again and then moved along the edge of her jaw, barely touching her skin. Her mind whirled, and for a moment she forgot why she had called him here. *Focus,* she told herself, before she allowed herself one more dizzying kiss.

Pulling back, she gasped for air. "Okay, wait. I mean, I have to think and I can't do it when you're doing that."

He ran a finger down the column of her throat. "Thinking is overrated."

"Stop!" Although she was laughing, she shoved him away with the tips of her fingers. He didn't budge.

"I'm serious, Justin. I called you because I need your help. I need you to help me on the O'Neil case."

"Let's leave him out of this for now," he answered. The smile went out of his eyes, like a blown-out candle.

"No, *listen to me.* Kyle said, 'You can see my mind in what I left behind.' Justin, there's something I'm missing. I feel it." Her hands rested on his shoulders, which stiffened beneath her touch. "Kyle's trying to send me a message that I can't see, and it's maddening. And when I was with Dr. Moore, I kept thinking about how we all have our jobs. I mean, each of us completes just one piece of the puzzle. I do bodies, you do crime scenes, we all have our little component so that our small cogs turn the great big wheel. But on Leather Ed's case you've had to keep things from me."

"That's because you're part of the case. If I give you access to the files I'm breaking the law."

"I know, but what if we—you and I—forget all that? What if we pool our resources? Share everything we've got? Dr. Moore thought my knowing was important. He already bent the rules, so I think you can, too."

"So you're saying two wrongs make a right?" The resistance was fading. She could feel him soften as he thought about this. She looked into his eyes and could almost see his mind click and whir as he turned the words over in his mind, but she could tell he had not yet committed to the idea. "Cammie, if this came out in a trial, it could hurt the case. I could lose my job."

"But I promise I won't tell a soul. I want you to show me the pictures in the file and tell me everything you found out about Leather Ed. And then we'll go to the histology and toxicology labs and we'll look over those files together. What if we stopped fighting and started sharing? Justin, I think we could catch him. Then we'd have more time together."

"Now you're not playing fair." He said this sternly, but his expression had resolved itself into amusement.

"I never said I did."

She waited, watching his face shift as he decided. He nodded, then took a slow step back. "I propose a compromise. Tomorrow's Valentine's Day."

"Yeah. It is," she answered, confused. "So what's the compromise?"

"If I do this, I want to pick up where we're leaving off right now. You're asking me to . . . redirect my energies. I'll say yes if you guarantee we'll be together tomorrow. Do we have a deal?"

"Deal," she said, and hugged him, feeling the muscles knot beneath his shirt. She quickly stepped back again, determined not to allow herself to get too distracted. "Okay," she said. "Let's get down to business. The case of Ed Staskiewicz as documented by the Silverton sheriff's office. Show me everything you've got."

Chapter Twelve

THE HISTOLOGY LAB was a strange mix of a room—both cluttered and clean. The cupboards had glass panels, and behind them Cameryn could see an array of bottles, while every inch of the counter space seemed to hold some piece of equipment or plastic file holders lined in a neat row. A single spider plant let down vines in the corner, the pot secured in a macramé holder knotted with wooden beads. White lab coats had been draped over the backs of office chairs; Dr. Moore sat in one chair, Cameryn's father in the other. Ben, who was perched on a tall stool, gave Cameryn a thumbs-up as she stepped inside.

"Well, you took your sweet time," her father said. His voice had a rumble to it, like the sound of a distant train.

"Sorry. We were . . . talking," Cameryn replied. She could feel her face flush as Justin moved close to her.

Patrick raised his eyebrows. "Hello, Justin."

Cameryn was surprised to see him reach out his hand toward Justin. Justin took it and pumped it twice. She couldn't help but think he looked sheepish as he said, "Hello, Mr. Mahoney."

"I will bow to the inevitable," her father replied. "Please, call me Patrick. Dr. Moore brought me up to speed on the tie-in with Leather Ed. This changes things," he said, his voice grim. "Kyle O'Neil is out of his mind. His insanity means he's bound to make a mistake. That's something for our side."

Justin was silent for a beat. He looked at Patrick as if he appreciated what he'd said, but he shook his head, saying, "He's not that kind of crazy, Mr.—Patrick. O'Neil's an organized killer. He's the kind of crazy who plans his every move in cold blood."

"But I think he *wants* to get caught," Cameryn argued. "Kyle's leaving clues."

"Or just playing with us," her father snapped. "In any event, Dr. Moore was kind enough to show me slides of the vic's lung tissue. The cause of death in all three cases is artificial pneumonia brought on by some unknown substance. What it is, I don't know, and *how* O'Neil did it is even more of a mystery. This case is as baffling as his last masterpiece using that klystron." He scratched the back of his neck and said, "It looks like bizarre deaths may be O'Neil's signature."

"I know, I thought about that, too, Dad; that's why I brought Justin in here. Kyle wants to be unique. He's showing off for the police. Or for me," she added hastily. "But he's left something for us to figure out and I want to try." Cameryn quickly explained her idea to everyone in the room, with various responses. Dr. Moore's face seemed as pugnacious as ever, but there was a curiosity, too, as he looked at Justin, considering. Her father frowned, while Ben seemed eager to try his hand at detective work. He nodded his head as she spoke.

"So we're gonna unravel us a mystery," Ben said, slapping his hands together to go all loose in the joints. "All right, what do we do first?"

"Let me show you the file on Leather Ed," Justin began. "Can we clear some space?"

"I'll get that desk." Hopping off the stool, Ben quickly rolled a computer desk with a laminate top and stopped it right in front of Justin.

"That'll work great," Justin told him. He laid the opened file on top and spread out the photographs in an arc, like a deck of cards. "Cameryn says we're missing something, and maybe she's right. I've already gone through this. While you study these, I'd like to take a look at those slides."

"Be my guest," said Dr. Moore. "That sample belongs to Leather Ed."

While Justin squinted into the microscope, Cameryn studied the glass rectangles, each one marked with a specific name. "Did you make these, Dr. Moore?"

"No, the slides are created here, in the histology lab. It's a process. You've seen me slice bits of tissue and place them in the cassettes—"

"Cassettes?" Cameryn asked. She frowned, trying to remember.

"Cassettes," he replied, a note of impatience in his voice. "Those small white plastic squares—you've seen them. They're on the table where I slice the organs. I put tiny chunks of heart, liver, lung, all the bits of visceral matter go into those containers. The lab technician takes the tissues to this lab and pours wax on top. Then they set. This device here"—he patted a square machine made of white enamel, with a huge, twelve-inch blade—"shaves the material that's embedded in the wax. Those slices are stained, heated, placed between glass slides, and voilà! We can examine the lung at a cellular level."

"I don't know what I'm looking at," Justin said and moved aside so that Cameryn could see. The image was cream colored with a ribbon of red circles touching one another in what looked like a string of beads.

"There's the foreign matter in the alveoli," Dr. Moore

murmured. "But for the life of me I can't say what it is."

Sighing, Cameryn pushed herself away from the microscope. Like Justin, she couldn't interpret it at all, which meant it was no use to her. She turned once again to the evidence reports, some printed out while others had been scrawled in ink. "Justin, what's all this?"

"That is everything we've got so far, including background information on Leather Ed. Plus a list of things found in his house. He served in Vietnam, bought the house and stayed in Silverton for over thirty years. But the guy was a loner. I realize I'm the new guy in town, but no one seems to have really known him."

Ben picked up a photograph of the living room and frowned. "Is this the inside of his house? Man, that place was a mess. That was one strange dude."

"I lived in Silverton all my life and I never really talked to him," Cameryn said, feeling a haze of guilt. In her mind's eye she saw him once again, hunched over his plate of food, his hair a mat of gray coils and his nails stained with tobacco. "He came into the Grand every so often and I served him, but now that I think about it, I don't even know what he did for a living." She stopped, considering this. "I mean, how did he pay his bills?"

Justin began rifling through the photographs. "I can't say for sure, but I know one thing he did that could have scored him some extra cash." Pulling a few pictures from the back of the pile, he said, "Look at this. Leather Ed grew pot. This was in his basement—the man was a regular horticulturalist. It could have been just for his own personal stash, but it's possible Leather Ed may have been dealing."

"You're *serious*?" Cameryn asked, genuinely shocked. She studied the various pictures of the basement. It was unceilinged and unpainted, with shelves overflowing with boxes of junk, rags, pipes, and tools, but in the center, sprouting from trays on a wooden table, grew row after row of marijuana plants. Above them hung a bank of grow lights, five-foot rectangles tacked to exposed wooden beams.

"So that is said cannabis. I've never actually seen it before."

"Very good, Cammie," her father told her, wagging shaggy brows at her. "As a father, I must say I'm encouraged. Perhaps, 'just say no' works after all."

"Dad, I would never touch the stuff," she assured him.

"But the thing is, Leather Ed wasn't just sparking bowls and pulling on blunts," Justin interrupted. "Look, we found a little bit of coke, too." He pointed to a picture of a box with small tinfoil squares shimmering at the bottom. "Those are called bindles. There's cocaine inside each one of those little packages."

"He had cocaine! Why didn't you tell me?" Cameryn demanded.

"Because you're not supposed to officially know about this case. We're bending all the rules here. Anyway, it doesn't seem like a big operation but might have been enough to generate some serious cash. Jacobs is tracing it down, trying to compare notes with the Durango squad. So far we don't have much of anything. It's still early in the investigation."

Cameryn narrowed her eyes. "Blunts? How do you know to call them 'blunts'?"

"It's street slang. Baby Bhang, Gold Star, Acapulco Red, Mota, Bambalacha—I worked in New York, remember? And in case you're wondering, I never inhaled." He laughed, but the sound died in his throat when he realized he was the only one who seemed amused. Dr. Moore thrust out his lower jaw, which made him look more like a bulldog than ever. He grunted from somewhere inside the folds of his neck.

His face shadowed with self-consciousness, Justin said, "That's a joke, by the way." He looked nervously from one set of eyes to another. "Seriously, I'm one of the good guys."

Ben's face, though, broke into a big, knowing smile. "It's cool, man. I lived in L.A. a while back. I've seen some crazy things, too."

"L.A., huh? So why'd you come all the way to Durango?"

"Probably the same reason you landed in Silverton. I like the small-town life. But even in the big city people didn't drown while they were sitting in a restaurant. This case is whack."

While the two of them talked, Cameryn picked up the photograph of Leather Ed in the chair. She concentrated on every detail, studying the shelves and the bit of curtain contained in the shot. Something was there. It tickled at the edge of her mind, taunting her, as though the idea was an image viewed through clouded glass. Every time she tried to grasp it, it seemed to slip away, the shadows shape-shifting, the thoughts turning more blurry. She bit the edge of her fingernail and asked, "Dr. Moore, did Leather Ed have pot or cocaine in his blood?"

"I have no idea." Dr. Moore spun a quarter turn in his chair so he was facing her. "The toxicology reports take time. They didn't make their way to my desk today, but it's possible the papers are still in the lab." He took off his glasses, polished them on the hem of his lab coat, then hooked them over his ears. "I'll go see if they're finished. I've got the key."

"That would be great," Cameryn answered.

He stood and offered her his chair, and when she sat in it she felt the warmth from his body.

"I told you before, Miss Mahoney, everything takes time. I'm willing to give you mine."

"Thanks, Dr. Moore. Really."

As the doctor disappeared through the door Cameryn pretended to be engrossed in the pictures, but inside she was bursting with gratitude for Dr. Moore. Time, the one thing he had so little of, was being freely donated to her when Dr. Moore could be home with his wife and children. Ben, too, had stayed, as had her father and, most important of all, Justin. The feeling of protection, of love, almost overwhelmed her. And yet there was a different kind of malignancy here, too. Kyle, as insidious as the cancer that was taking Dr. Moore's life, needed to be cut out, and there was only one way to do it. She had to think her way through. The answer was there, if only she could see it.

Once again, she picked up a photograph of Leather Ed sitting in the chair. The book was in his lap, held in place by skeletonized fingertips. Cameryn's ponytail fell in the way so she flicked it behind her back. Turning the photograph every which way, she tried to read the print, but it was no use.

"What is it, Cammie?" Ben asked. "You see something?"

"I'm not sure. Justin? Do you remember what kind of book this was?"

"I think it had something to do with plants. It's still in the cooler."

"Is there any chance you could bring it in here so I could get a look at it? I think that says page 203."

Justin shrugged. "Sure, I can get it, but if you touch

the book you'll have to wear gloves. I'll grab us a couple of pairs from the autopsy suite." He turned to Ben. "Do you have evidence tape? We'll have to cut the bag open and reseal it with my name and date, so I'll need fresh tape."

"Sure. It's put away but I'll go with you and grab it out of the drawer. You know, I've never worked on this end of things before, and I got to say I'm curious to see how it's done."

Snorting, Justin said, "That's the thing—it's never done like this. This is all Cammie, all the way."

"Yeah," Ben agreed. "It's all about bending the rules. We'll do whatever it takes."

"And I," Cameryn said, shooting a look that was deadly serious, "am all about saving Justin. You keep forgetting that Kyle typed your name, too. This isn't just about me anymore."

"I can take care of myself," Justin growled.

"How about this? We'll save each other."

In spite of himself, Justin grinned. "All right, Cammie. I guess I can live with that."

She could hear their voices trail away as they made their way down the hall. Now only Cameryn and her father remained in the lab. From the corner of her eye she saw Patrick lean toward her in his chair, his large hands clasped between his knees. He was not heavy but solid, and today he was wearing a clan

Aran sweater knit in the Mahoney clan pattern. Her mammaw had made it out of natural wool, a color her grandmother called báinín. In the middle there was a diamond row, representing a wish for wealth, flanked by two cables that symbolized luck, and next to it she'd created a link that stood for the unbroken chain between the Irish who emigrated and those who remained at home.

Absently, her father began to rub his fingers along the luck cable. "I'm beginning to like Justin," he said.

"Me, too," she replied. The book intrigued her, as did the plants. "Dad, how long do you think Leather Ed was dead in that chair?"

"Three weeks, more or less."

"The automatic food and water dog dish probably held about a three-week food supply, so that timeline fits. And there's the outline the note left on the table. Which in itself is kind of weird because the house was a sty. So Kyle must have dusted before putting down the note. But why would he do that?"

She could feel her father watching her as she flipped from photograph to photograph, and although she tried to ignore it she could feel her father's eyes boring into her. Finally, exasperated, she set down the photographs and said, "Dad! Why are you staring?"

There was a pause characteristic of her father. "I'm looking at my daughter," he answered.

"A daughter who is trying to concentrate. I can't do it if you're watching me." Once again she turned her attention to Leather Ed and the pale green plants that bloomed next to his side. Slanting her eyes, she tried to read the top line of the book. If she rotated it just right, she could maybe make out the word *hydration*. A little further she teased out *polymer* and *crystals*.

It almost startled her when her father spoke again. "I'm looking at my daughter and thinking she's not the same anymore."

"What's that supposed to mean?"

He didn't answer. Sighing, she let her hand with the photograph drift to her lap, because she knew there was something he wanted to say to her that couldn't wait. His white hair had been combed back, gelled in place so that the teeth of the comb left tiny furrows. Judge Amy Green, the woman he was dating in Ouray, had reinvented Cameryn's father. Instead of heavy work boots, he now wore cowboy boots made with tooled leather. The denim on his jeans was never faded, the hem no longer frayed. While she had to admit he looked more polished, she somehow missed the bear of the man he'd once been. Nothing ever stayed in place, though. Everything in life shifted like sand beneath a tide.

"When I wasn't looking, you grew up on me," said her father. "It happened and I didn't even see it."

"Yeah, well, a couple of death threats will do that."

"This isn't funny, Cameryn. This whole thing is surreal. We're sitting here, going over evidence left by a killer, and you're so . . . mature. How are you doing it?"

"I guess it's the Irish in me. I mean, we're tough, don't you think? And it's not like you haven't changed, Dad. Look at you, all fancy now."

"You're not a girl anymore, are you." The way he said it made it a statement, not a question.

How was she supposed to answer that? "But that's a good thing, right? If you do your job right then I *should* grow. I mean, life's different for both of us; Mom's back in New York and you've got Amy now. And I've got Justin. Everything keeps moving and changing, like it's supposed to."

He seemed to think about this. "Your mammaw always said it's our job to grow. She said we water our family with love."

At that moment Dr. Moore came in holding the reports in his hand. Without looking up he said, "There's cocaine in all of their systems, but not enough to be even near a lethal dose. . . ." He stopped, registering Cameryn's expression, which had frozen into place. "What's going on?" Dr. Moore asked. "Miss Mahoney, you look like you've seen a ghost."

Grow. Water. The words reverberated in her mind. She felt her eyes grow wide as the pieces snapped into place, the mosaic no longer scrambled but reassembled into a discernible pattern. Could the answer be something so easy, yet as deadly as that? It was so simple, really. In that instant she knew she had the answer. It had been staring her in the face all along.

"That's it. Water. It's the water!" She could feel her hands begin to shake as she looked at the photograph in her hands.

Her father looked at her, confused. Dr. Moore, too, frowned in disbelief. "I fail to understand . . ." Dr. Moore began, but Cameryn cut him off. Waving the picture, she said, "Look at that plant! It's blooming— its petals opening without having been watered. You said Leather Ed sat there for three weeks, right? That's three weeks without water. Those plants should have withered. All of the plants in that house should have died, including the marijuana. But they *didn't*. And the book—the book Leather Ed is holding says *polymer crystals*. You know—*polymer* crystals! They're used for plant hydration."

Patrick shook his head, confused. "I'm sorry, you're saying you figured this out because of what was in the water? I—I don't understand."

"No, Dad! It's because of what was in the *soil*."

Dr. Moore grabbed the photograph out of her hand. She could see the glint of understanding in his eyes. "It's possible, Miss Mahoney. More than possible. And it would explain everything," he said so loud he was practically shouting. "The texture, the gel, I've seen it but I never made the connection. Of course, cocaine is inhaled, so that would give a reason as to how it got into the lungs." He was talking fast now, his words rapid-fire. "All three had low levels of cocaine in their blood, so all three inhaled a substance. If the drug was cut with the polymer then it would expand instantly in the lungs, pulling water from their own tissue. They would drown in their own body fluid."

"And if Leather Ed was dealing, it would explain how it got to Safer and Stein," Cameryn said, addressing her comments only to him. "The gel would coat the alveoli—"

"—causing instant suffocation," Moore announced. "That is exactly how they presented in death. All three men."

"Will one of you two slow down and tell me what is going on?" Patrick cried.

But this was a moment that was for just the two of them, for Dr. Moore and Cameryn. She could feel the invisible thread wind around them both again, pulling them together, tighter, like a filament alive with the electricity of shared knowledge.

"Of course, the next step is to get a control sample and run it through the gas chromatograph. That's when we'll know for certain." Moore looked at her, beaming, with triumph in his eyes. "But I'm putting my money on you, Miss Mahoney. You're not just my protégée," he said. "You're my legacy."

Chapter Thirteen

"LUCKY GUESS," JUSTIN teased her from her kitchen doorway. "Unbelievably lucky guess."

"No," Cameryn said, yawning, "I'm a genius. Mammaw says so."

"I do indeed," said her grandmother. "Here, Justin, let me take your coat. And have a seat. There's fresh coffee and a pound cake, or if you'd like I can make you breakfast, although it's past ten. Herself there just barely got up. And oh, those flowers are lovely—I'll put them in water for Cammie."

Justin, who held a large bouquet of pink and red roses, broke the bundle in two. "These," he said, holding out the pink ones, "are for you. Happy Valentine's Day."

Her grandmother smiled, like sunshine bursting.

"Why, isn't that something! Flowers for me. It's been years . . . but you shouldn't be spending your money on such things. It's an extravagance, especially roses. Never do such a thing again." From her grandmother's expression Cameryn knew she didn't mean it. Wearing a red jogging suit that zipped up to her chin, Mammaw moved lightly in her slippers. From a cupboard beneath the sink she produced two vases, a clear one and one that looked like green marble. "Which would you like, Cammie?" she asked.

"The clear."

"Perfect. I prefer the green." Immediately Mammaw began to snip the bottoms of the stems with kitchen shears. Justin was watching her closely. When her back was turned he swooped down and gave Cameryn a kiss on her mouth.

His skin was still cool from being outside, but his lips were warm against hers. She wanted him to linger but he pulled away, whispering "Later" so softly she was sure Mammaw couldn't hear. The second bundle, which had been thrust behind his back, suddenly reappeared, and Cameryn could tell right away they were the expensive kind. A thick rose fragrance emanated from every bloom, and, wrapped in cellophane sprinkled with pink hearts, this bundle was twice as big as the one he'd given Mammaw. He dropped into the kitchen chair next to her. "It's a lucky break that

Valentine's Day is a Saturday this year, because I'm off duty. And I've made plans." His eyes looked green in the morning light.

"Thank you so much for these," Cameryn replied, drinking in the fragrance. "But—what kind of plans? I'm supposed to stay in the house. I was only let out yesterday because I was with my dad."

"Let's just say I got clearance. Nice jammies, by the way. Penguins?" One dark eyebrow rose on his forehead.

"I like penguins," Cameryn answered, suddenly aware of how non-Valentine she looked in her blue flannel bottoms and knit top. "Lyric gave these to me for Christmas. And if you would have called first I would have taken a shower and gotten myself pulled together. You drop by, this is what you get."

"I wasn't complaining." He was out of uniform, in jeans and a Broncos sweatshirt, and he seemed both amused and happy. "You wear penguins better than anyone. And I like your hair down like that. It's so long, almost like a waterfall." Reaching out, he touched her hair, but her grandmother looked over her shoulder and Justin quickly withdrew his hand.

"Thanks. That was a very Valentiney thing to say," Cameryn whispered.

"I would like to say more," he whispered back. "Alone."

"Did you say you wanted coffee, Justin?" asked Mammaw.

"Yes, thanks. Anyway, before I get too off track, I want to tell you how amazed everyone is with Cammie's mind." Clasping his hands together, he placed them behind his neck and leaned back, balancing on the chair's back legs, something she was never allowed to do. But if her grandmother noticed she didn't say a word as she set a red mug filled with coffee onto the heart-shaped place mat before she bustled back to the sink and her roses.

"Amber says Cameryn is a savant and Jacobs wants you to ditch forensics and go into law."

Cameryn felt herself beam. "So they got a match!"

"Yep. The gas chromatograph results came back a total hit. Looks like Leather Ed did a bit of business in Telluride, which is where Safer and Stein must have scored their bags. It's already been on the news, so hopefully users will toss their drugs. Who knows how many of those things were tainted?"

"Gas chroma—what?" her grandmother asked. Turning from the counter with a rose poised in her hand, she waved it like a baton. "I have to confess I'm still not clear at all on what happened last night. Patrick tried to explain before he left, but I'm not sure even he understands. So please, speak slow and use small words."

Justin glanced at Cameryn, his eyes twinkling. "Basically, your granddaughter looked at the pictures of the crime scene and put the pieces together."

"Part of the credit goes to you, Mammaw," Cameryn interrupted. "I remembered how you put those polymer crystals in the soil, you know, so the dirt would hold on to the water longer. You used them in your flower boxes."

"Yes, those crystals are quite the thing," her grandmother agreed. The rose now wagged in her hand, the bloom bouncing like the head of a doll on a spring. "The church did a craft project using jelly jars—we put food coloring, fragrance, water, and crystals all together and sold them at the fair. Remember?"

"No," Cameryn said. She made it a point to avoid craft fair projects with her grandmother.

"Well, I'm not surprised, it was years ago. The thing that amazed me was that one little teaspoon of the crystals would soak up enough water to fill the entire jar. A crystal smaller than a pea would swell to the size of an ice cube. So . . ." She jabbed the rose into the vase. "Let me tell you what I know from your father. I understand that Kyle ground the crystals into a powder. I also understand that he cut that powder into Leather Ed's cocaine. Poor, lost soul, I never knew he was into such things," she muttered, sticking three more roses in to make a pink halo. "But what I don't understand is how you, Cammie, figured it out. How did you do it, girl?"

"It's not that big of a deal—I just noticed the plants didn't die," Cameryn said simply. "And the book—"

"That part was *amazing*." The chair came down with a thud as Justin broke into an even wider grin. "The book was opened to the page that talked about putting polymer into soil. Cammie noticed it when none of us did. Kyle left us a clue but we missed it. Cameryn didn't."

"And the gas—thingamajig. What is that?" Her grandmother frowned.

"Gas chromatograph—that's a machine that tells what a substance is made of. The guys in the lab had already run a sample from all three of our vics' lungs, but here's the thing: the result came back as *unknown*. There was no match in the system. Moore said it would have taken weeks, maybe months, to figure out what the jelly stuff was, because there was nothing in the database to compare it to. But once they put the polymer crystals in the test tube they got a perfect hit. All thanks to your granddaughter."

"She's a wonder, that one," her grandmother agreed. "Would you like me to put your roses in a vase?" she asked, and Cameryn quickly agreed. She had other plans that included Justin, away from her mammaw's prying eyes.

"Um, Mammaw, can I show Justin something I made him? It's in my room."

"What? Of course," her grandmother agreed. "Leave your door open," trailed after her as Cameryn pulled Justin upstairs, glad she'd at least brushed her teeth. They were barely inside her doorway when he turned her around, pressing her back into her wall as he kissed her, and Cameryn almost giggled at first because he was so daring, before the laughter died and her thoughts once again turned blurry at the edges.

That was the power he'd taught her—to choose which trail she would mentally follow. Kyle, the horrible murders, the polymers, all were pushed back into the furthest places of her mind and she would choose this joy, this sensation that obliterated the dark. It was Valentine's Day, and Justin had brought her roses, and a kind of bubbly happiness fizzed inside her with its own effervescence. She wanted to wrap herself inside this good feeling. For a moment he broke free, leaning away so he could look her in the eye, but she pursued him. Bouncing onto the tips of her toes, she pulled him back and kissed him again, noting the slightly abrasive feel of his unshaved skin against her lips. Then he was hugging her, laughing softly as she clung to him.

"Excuse me, Justin, what is so funny?"

He rested his chin on the top of her head. "Because

I have studied body language—I know what people do when they're lying, and you just told a whopper to your mammaw."

"I don't know what you're talking about."

"Really? Then what did you 'make' me?" He made a pretense of looking around the room.

"Okay, I didn't actually *make* you anything," she admitted. "I *was* going to get you something but then things got all crazy and I didn't get a chance. So I confess, I wanted to get you alone. Lying is a venial sin, not a mortal one, right? Believe it or not, I'm not sure anymore."

"It's a venial sin."

"So I won't burn in hell?"

He placed a finger over her lips, hushing her. "Cammie, you are the best present of all."

For a moment he reset his gaze on her eyes, and then once again his lips found hers and time seemed to bend so that she couldn't quite track where she was in space. The music downstairs was a part of it, the soft fluted notes of Celtic music her grandmother had put on, the snipping sound the shears made as she cut the red roses, the way Justin's hands cupped the sides of her face. His fingers wound through her hair just as she heard it, the sound that penetrated into her brain, like a wrong note. It was a *ping*, coming from her computer.

"Justin," she said, her voice tight. "Wait. Did you hear that?"

He registered her shifting mood immediately. "What?"

"My computer."

She didn't have to say more. Justin's gaze snapped over to her screen. Her computer was on, just as Andrew had told her to leave it, but the screen saver shimmered across the screen like waves of water blotting out the message.

"Lyric?"

"Maybe. But she knows what's going on, that everything is being watched. I don't think it's Lyric."

Justin pushed her behind him, as if the danger were on the screen itself. Together they walked toward the desk, Cameryn trailing by a half step, the feeling of dread spreading through her as the screen loomed large. Before he went to the computer he snapped her curtains shut. Then he reached over and shook the mouse. "Stop hiding, you bastard," he said in a voice so hard Cameryn barely recognized it as Justin's. Instantly, the screen saver vanished, and there, in the prearranged chat room, were the words that made the blood turn to water in her veins.

Happy Valentine's Day, my anam cara. *I want to be sure this is you and not the police. What was the shape of my grandmother's tombstone? I showed it to you in the cemetery.*

Staring at the screen with single-minded ferocity, Justin demanded, "Cameryn, do you know the answer?"

She nodded, her heart thrumming in her chest. Clutching the back of her chair, she felt her legs wobble. She looked at the screen, and then up at Justin, but he was already punching numbers into his phone.

"Cammie, type back to him," he ordered. "We've got to keep him going." On the phone, he began to talk to Sheriff Jacobs, looking sharply from the screen to the window and then to Cameryn while he fired off commands as though it were he, and not the sheriff, who was in charge.

She found she couldn't move. Wide-eyed, she stared at the screen. Justin turned to her, his lips pressed into a hard line. How had her body seized up like that, to disconnect her mind from her flesh? Placing a hand on each of her shoulders, he pulled her closer to him, ever so slightly.

"I know you're scared—I understand. Tell me what to write and I'll do it for you," he told her. "Please." He looked at her with such a focused intensity that she found herself coming back. It was like following a beacon in a lighthouse. "Andrew is coming right now. Tell me the shape of his grandmother's tombstone and I'll type the words. You don't have to do a thing. Cammie, Kyle won't hurt you. I won't let him."

"I can do it." Her voice sounded far away.

"Mrs. Mahoney!" he bellowed. "Call Patrick. O'Neil has just made contact. The police are on their way."

"Oh my God." She heard her grandmother's soft cry.

Justin was about to sit in the chair but Cameryn sank into it first. "I said I can do it." Her fingers were shaking so hard it was difficult to type out the words.

I'm here. It's me, Cammie. The tombstone looked like the pages on an open book. What do you want?

The message was delivered instantly. A second later, and she read his response.

You.

Justin cursed under his breath. Jerking his hands through his hair, he said, "Tell him you know he killed Leather Ed. Ask him why he did it."

Obedient, Cameryn transcribed Justin's words.

A moment later she read:

I knew it would get your attention. I heard the warning on the news for the druggies to dump their cocaine, so I figured you got my little messages I left. I hope it was you who figured it out. I remember how much you like puzzles.

Her fingers flew over the keyboard without Justin's prompting.

You are insane. You said you did not kill Brent Safer and Joseph Stein and now I know you did.

A heartbeat later he wrote:

They were collateral damage. I am NOT insane, Cam-

*mie. I am like you. I think that part scares you—finding
that we are the same person. And before you condemn
me for killing a man, be aware that I listened to you.
This time I chose a person less important than Brad
Oakes. Leather Ed was a waste of skin. He was a drug
dealer. I hardly think he'll be missed. Don't you think
it's fun playing together again?*

Justin's words were like bullets. "What is *collateral
damage*? Ask him why he killed Safer and Stein."

The message had barely been sent when Kyle's
words chimed back.

*Their deaths were pure, random chance. I broke
into Leather Ed's and toyed with his drugs. It was like
a lottery ticket, you know? I mixed in only a few bad
bags with the good. Then I watched to see what would
happen. It was wild that one of the men who ended
up with my concoction was a BIG celebrity. There is a
truth in that: the rich die just like the poor. Leather Ed
snorted his last line in his room, sitting in his chair,
while I waited in his basement. He didn't know what
hit him.*

Another *ping* sounded just as they finished reading.
Is Justin with you?

Cameryn whipped around to look at Justin, who
in turn shook his head hard. "Tell him no." His voice
cracked like breaking ice.

No.

And then the one word typed back:

Liar.

At that point she heard a commotion at her front door, then her mammaw leading Andrew the FBI agent and Sheriff Jacobs up the stairs, their boots matching the pounding of her heart. Justin quickly filled them in on what was happening, finishing up by saying, "I don't know what to do now. It may be a bluff or O'Neil might be watching." The panic was rising in his voice. "My goal was to keep him communicating but I can't see my way to the next move."

It was Andrew who took control. In a calm voice, he said, "Deputy, you did a fine job. We've got our people tracking him but it's going to be next to impossible now that he's using the chat room."

"What's the answer, then?" asked Jacobs. Cameryn could hear their voices behind her, but she didn't turn around. As she watched their shadow images flicker across the screen, her mind pulsed against the one word. *Liar.* Did Kyle know she was surrounded by people, or was he somewhere far away, playing games?

"We need to get him to use a phone," Andrew said. "We've checked the inventory of Leather Ed's belongings and his cell phone is missing. Our guess is that O'Neil's got it. Try to have him call you on that phone, Cameryn. We can track it if you do."

Now she did turn around. "How am I going to get him to do that?"

Andrew was dressed down today, in khakis and a tan shirt. His hair looked silver in the light, his jaw more square. "I want you to type exactly what I'm going to tell you to say. Are you ready to catch him?"

"Yes."

"You're a brave girl. Now, the first thing I want you to do is to type to him that you really care about him."

Cameryn gasped, balking at the idea. *"No!"*

"You've got to get him to trust you," Andrew said. He was leaning close to her shoulder, and she could smell the faintest whiff of aftershave. "Write down a memory you two shared, then tell him you are worried about what will happen to him. We'll do this one piece at a time."

"Justin?" She looked to him for confirmation, but he nodded in agreement.

"Do it," he said. "If we catch him it'll be over."

She searched her memory, trying to find a strand she could pull from her memories with Kyle, thoughts she'd tried so hard to forget.

Do you remember when we were in the church and I told you about my mother? I told you all about Hannah. I told you how she left me when I was little, and you sat and listened to me.

"Good, good," Andrew crooned. "Keep going."

I think you understood how hard that was. I know your mom left you, too. Kyle, you have to be careful. You could get killed.

She swallowed hard before adding a line that was a lie that was not venial, but mortal. A black mark on her soul. *I don't know what I'd do if you got hurt.*

Patting her shoulder, Andrew said, "Perfect. You need to connect with him in a way that makes him feel safe. We've got to get his guard down. Send it."

She did.

That's just the thing, Cammie. I don't care anymore. I've played the game and I've won. There's nothing left for me now.

Andrew looked excited. With darting movements he assessed the room, then made a steeple with his hands, crossing his thumbs, and tapped his fingers against his pursed lips. "He's showing vulnerability. That's exactly what we want. Keep him typing. We have to go slow and draw him out carefully. This is all about strategy."

Andrew droned on in her ear as Cameryn, compliant, typed the words. She wrote that what Kyle did was in some ways understandable. That it must be hard to live apart from everyone else, and for the first time she, Cammie, could see the world from his side. She told him he was not alone. Back and forth, back and forth, they typed for an hour, then two. Justin paced behind her while she transcribed, urging her to add personal details wherever they fit so that Kyle knew the words were coming from her. Her father arrived, too worried to say anything, his paw of a hand resting on the top of her head before he sat in a chair to watch the drama unfold. The female CBI agent, Chris, kept up a constant stream of talk over the phone with a judge who was waiting to grant a warrant at a moment's notice. The muscles in Cameryn's back were a mass of knots as she wrote words she did not believe. Her fingers, at first cold, had slowly turned to ice.

Give yourself up. Please. It's the only way.

That message was repeated in various ways, just as Andrew told her to do. And, exactly as he predicted, Kyle's writing became more personal. He spoke of his rage, his despair, the sense of apartness he felt from the rest of the human race. He told her of his crushing loneliness and the fact that only she understood his need for death, because she, too, was drawn to that place; it was a rope, he said, that would lead them both back to the living. The last line he wrote was that he loved her. He typed the words again and again.

"All right, I think we've got him where we want him." Andrew's voice could barely contain his excitement. He pointed to the screen. "It's showtime. Tell him you want to hear his voice. Tell him you *need* to hear it."

Kyle, I want to talk to you. I need to hear your voice.

She felt as though someone had physically punched her in the gut. The message back took longer this time:

The minutes on my phone are gone. I bought a disposable phone and the minutes are gone. We have to type.

"This is it," Andrew said. He took a deep breath and blew it between his teeth. "Tell him to use Leather Ed's. If he forgets we can trace a regular cell phone, we got him. Try, Cammie."

Please call me on Leather Ed's phone. I know you have it. I need to talk to you. It's important that I hear your voice even if it's only for a minute.

She stared at her blank screen. Everyone had crowded inside her small room and she could feel their collective body heat; her grandmother, her father, Andrew, Chris, Sheriff Jacobs, and Justin, each quietly waiting on pins and needles. Justin stood behind her, his hands gripping her shoulders as he stared, expectant, at the screen. "He's not answering. Maybe we scared him off," he said softly. "Maybe we pushed too hard."

"We had to make our move," Andrew replied. "The cell phone is our only hope. Chris has a judge at the ready. We'll have the warrant within seconds and we can trace the cell phone using locater pings. The guy needs to call. Just one mistake." His voice dropped to a whisper. "Pick up the phone, O'Neil. Call. Just call."

And then, like an answer to prayer, Cameryn's BlackBerry went off in her back pocket. The spit had dried in her mouth, as she held up the screen and said the two words she never wanted to say. "It's him."

Chapter Fourteen

CAMERYN PACED BACK and forth in front of Justin's desk, anxious and infuriated by his apparent calm. He was in his too-small office chair, one finger pressed in his ear as he spoke to Sheriff Jacobs. His feet were propped on his desk, the tips of his boots so scuffed they resembled sandpaper.

"How close are you?" He waited a moment before replying, "Good. No, she's fine. Nervous, of course, but keeping her here with me is the right thing to do. Yeah, I'll tell her. Let me know the second you arrest him."

"Tell me what?" she demanded as soon as the phone returned to the hook.

"That they've still got the signal loud and strong. It's coming from the Old Hundred Mine, which is exactly where O'Neil said he was. The police will be there in less than five minutes."

"Five minutes." She resumed pacing. "What if he's not there?"

"Not possible. While you were talking to him the FBI was able to run a locator trace, which went right to Leather Ed's cell phone. He's there, Cammie. The entire cavalry is descending on the Old Hundred Mine right now. Oh, and the sheriff also told me to tell you that even though it's hard, you need to relax. Everything is under control."

"Relax." She snorted, then made another round through the ten-foot-square floor space, her hiking boots thudding against the worn wood. She'd changed out of her pajamas in the bathroom instead of her bedroom since there were so many strangers crowded around her desk. Her choice had been simple: the jeans she wore to school a few times a week, worn and faded at the knees, her hiking boots, a pair of cotton socks, a blue tee shirt. It was her top, plucked from a closet shelf, that had been out of character. For the first time she'd chosen her Mahoney clan sweater, the twin of her father's, the one her mammaw had made. It had never been Cameryn's style before that exact moment. But today, with so much of her life unraveling around her she wanted to wear the symbol for luck, the emblem of survival knitted into the Aran wool. It itched where it touched her bare skin, and the muslin-colored yarn had a faint, unique odor, as though it contained the barest trace of wet sand. She looked at the double row of knitted cables, fingering them as her father had on his own. Today she needed all the luck she could get. All of them did.

She heard Justin's chair squeak as he set his feet firmly on the floor. "Cammie, you need to calm down."

Glaring at him, she snapped, "I already told you I hate it when people tell me that!"

"Oh, yeah. Right." Justin had the grace to look sheepish.

"There is so much adrenaline pouring through me right now I feel like I need to move. What I don't understand is how you can just sit there. I mean, I just did something crazy."

"Could you be a little more specific?"

She shot him a look.

Justin rolled his eyes. "That was meant to be funny, by the way, and you didn't even crack a grin. I must be losing my touch."

"No, I'm just losing my mind." She looked at the phone and bit her lip so hard she tasted blood. "Why don't they call?"

"They *will*. Everything's going to be fine."

"How much longer?"

Justin looked at his watch and sighed. "Sixty seconds closer since the last time you asked, so . . . four minutes. More or less."

The office was too small to get in more than six good strides, so it took her only moments to complete a circle.

"Don't let him get into your head," he told her softly.

"That's just the thing—I can't get him *out*!" She shook herself as though she could dislodge the thoughts, but there was no way to loosen them because they were inside her. Kyle's wrenching sobs reverberated through her mind like the echo from a bell.

In the end, Kyle had agreed to turn himself in because of her.

"Are you sure I should do this, Cammie? Give myself up?" he'd pleaded.

"Yes," she'd said, reading Andrew's hastily written notes. "It's for the best. You'll get all the help you need. And I promise, no one will hurt you. Trust me."

That had been the point where Kyle had finally relented. He'd said yes to her while Andrew, pumping his fist in triumph, mouthed the words *We've got him!*

"I'll turn myself in," Kyle finally told her. His voice was thick, and she heard him pause to catch his breath. "But you have to be there. Promise me, my *anam cara*."

Tell him yes, Andrew had written. *Tell him anything he wants. We've located the ping. Keep him talking.*

And so she'd promised as though her life depended on it. She had wondered, listening to him weep, if there was still a spark of a soul inside him as he claimed. Had she really caused the flame of humanity to grow, or were those the soulless words of a madman? How would he feel when he learned she had lied to him? Did it even matter? From that thought she turned away.

"Cammie, don't think about it anymore."

Whirling around, she could feel her eyes go wide. "Like I've got some switch inside that I can turn on or off! You're not the one who talked to him. You didn't have to actually hear Kyle cry over the phone. I had to pretend I actually cared. I'm not an actress, Justin. I had to lie when he told me that I was his *anam cara*. That's what Andrew told me to do and I did it. Lie and lie and lie." She felt her stomach heave with her emotions, as if she were walking on the deck of a ship caught in roiling waves. "I feel horrible!"

Justin sat up, and faster than she would have thought possible he was on his feet, pulling her close. "Shhh," he said into her hair. "You're right, this whole thing has been hardest on you." She felt a light kiss on the crown of her head. Inside she felt as tight as wire, the panic pulling her so thin she was afraid she would snap into pieces that would curl away like ribbons.

"Cammie, it's going to be okay. I told you before. We'll get him."

"But I want you to promise," she whispered. Her breathing was ragged as she swallowed back panic.

"Promise me they'll get him and I can forget about all of this death?"

"Yes, Cammie, I promise." She could feel how strong Justin's arms were. Stronger than she'd known.

His voice was husky as he said, "You did good getting him to use the phone of Leather Ed's. That was the key. You need to stay tough and get through this last little bit."

"I did everything Andrew said and I'm not sure it was right."

"Of course it was right. Andrew is with the FBI. He knew exactly what to do and you did it and it worked. Quit trying to second-guess yourself, Cammie. Let someone else carry the load now, okay?"

Cameryn looked at the office door's small pane of glass. SHERIFF'S OFFICE was stenciled in black, along with a gold star. Shadow figures moved past the rippled glass, and she thought how strange it was that life for them went on, that it went on for everyone, even though hers had been placed on pause. The shadow people in the hallway were there on business, tying up the threads of their everyday lives in a courthouse that was the heartbeat of the town, oblivious to the drama playing inside this small room. She wished for their blissful ignorance.

But she was finding strength inside herself, too, siphoning it off Justin and pulling it up from the depths of her own soul. As she stood, her body pressed into his, she could feel it. She felt herself coming back together as her breathing slowed. Of course Justin was right. She had to take the step to trust someone else, to let the police do their job.

He'd been so good to her through this, a rock. In her mind's eye she tried to see her path with him but it was as cloudy as the images behind the glass. There was no way to guess where they would end up, but for once she didn't require herself to scientifically solve the equation, to have the answer neatly filled out on the page in the certainty of black and white. Here, listening to his heart thud beneath his jersey, encircled by his protecting arms, she could just *be*.

"Are you okay now?" he asked. He pulled his head back so he could look into Cameryn's face.

"Better."

"Good." He smiled, but it was cautious, like someone sticking a toe in the water to check out the temperature. "You're sure?"

"Did you know there are people out there? In the hallway. Why are they here on a Saturday?"

Relief sparked in his eyes and she figured her outburst must have really scared him. "Because the Silverton County Courthouse is a happening place," he said with forced cheer.

"Yeah." Cameryn managed a small smile. "It holds the sheriff's office—"

"—which is right next to the Motor Vehicle Registration Office, which is next to the Clerk Recorder. We are big-time city now, open for a half day on Saturday." He stepped away from her, holding her elbow to make sure she was steady on her feet. "Look, I'll do whatever I can to make this easier on you. How about I call the sheriff again and get an update?"

"That would be great. Don't tell him I'm freaking out, though. I don't want anyone to know."

"Freaking out is a secret held between you and me. And go ahead and start pacing again if it will help. Just don't wear the shine off the floor. Have mercy on this old building. It's an antique."

Cameryn knew how true that was. The sheriff's office was nestled in the center of the county courthouse, a gray stone building built in tiers with a gray slate roof. The cement stairs leading up to the building were guarded by pillars that supported a widow's walk. A large clock tower was topped by a golden dome, a Victorian touch, of which many Silverton residents seemed inordinately proud. Inside the building was a small lobby protected by a wall of glass honeycombed with wire, and beyond that ran a wide wooden hallway Cameryn knew well. Various governmental departments were accessible from either side of the corridor, their names stenciled in the same block letters on identical glass panes. The sheriff's office, halfway down the hallway on the left, consisted of a small outer office with two desks. Behind the office was an another chamber that contained a single jail cell. The cell that would hold Kyle.

She began to pace, slower this time, as he dialed. They heard a sharp rap on the glass that made them both jump. The doorknob jiggled but didn't open since Justin had locked it. Still holding the cordless phone, Justin made his way cautiously to the door and peered through the glass.

"FedEx," he said as he tossed her the phone, which she caught easily in her hand. "Cammie, you talk to Jacobs while I get this—"

He didn't say any more.

Cameryn saw the blade before Justin did, his head turned ninety degrees toward her as the sentence died in his throat. Was that what had cost him, the looking at her? In that second she saw the slash of silver and the spurt of blood. She stood frozen. What she saw could not be happening. It was impossible. And yet it was.

Time did indeed slow to a crawl right before death.

She had read about the phenomenon of the near-dead, the way seconds stretched into minutes when the end of life flashed before a victim. What she hadn't known was the same rule applied when you watched someone else in the throes of dying. Each millisecond became a second, each second an eternity.

The blade was long, curved at the end, and the thrust was instantaneous and hard. It took only a moment for the weapon to pierce Justin's ribs, and a moment more for the sick sound of steel cutting flesh as the blade jerked up. She'd heard Justin's sharp intake of breath and a hiss of air escaping. Wide-eyed, he'd looked at Cameryn as though he didn't understand what had happened, his mind too slow to comprehend. The man used the thrust of his knife to push Justin back into the office, where he collapsed onto the floor, a disjointed bundle of legs and arms, as though someone had cut a marionette's strings. Justin's eyes rolled back into his head. Blood, black against his jersey, spread scarlet onto the floor. With a chortle, the man stepped inside and looked at her with a smile just discernible beneath the bill of his FedEx cap.

"Hello, Cammie," he said, flipping off the cap.

In a dream, in a nightmare, she saw the aquiline nose, the glittering, controlled anger that appeared in Kyle O'Neil's hazel eyes. Quickly, he shut the door behind him.

"You promised you'd be there for me when I turned myself in. But you lied." His voice, cool as winter wind, was just above a whisper. "Don't worry, I knew you would. I'm an Eagle Scout, remember? I'm always prepared. Which is more than I can say for your boyfriend here." He kicked Justin's body with the toe of his boot.

"Don't make a sound or I'll cut him again."

Could he tell she was going to scream? She could feel it surge inside her, a bubble of horror rising up, ready to burst out of her throat. Staring at the knife, she registered the blade, scarlet with Justin's blood as he lay twitching on the ground.

"You look surprised to see me. Aren't you going to say hello? I thought I meant something to you and you don't even extend me a common courtesy."

Justin, stabbed. Justin, dying.

And then her body unlocked itself and she screamed, flailing toward Justin, but Kyle grabbed her arm so hard she thought for a moment he'd cut her, too.

"Not him," he hissed. "Me. Come on, Cammie. Our own little adventure is about to begin."

Chapter Fifteen

THE COUPLE COMING toward her in the county courthouse hallway might save her! Their footsteps reverberating thunderously along the honeyed wood, the woman, her hair cut short and spiked, leaned her head against the man, whose own hair hung in a dark braid. Cameryn's heart beat so loud in her ears it almost drowned out any other sound, and she wondered if someone outside her body could actually hear the panic she felt. But the couple, too engrossed in each other, took no notice as they approached.

"Shhh," Kyle breathed into her ear in a sickening mimicry of Justin's soothing whisper. And then, as though he and Cammie were involved in a conversation, he said loud enough for the couple to hear, "FedEx delivers on Saturdays but we charge a heck of a lot more for the service." He kept his voice light, conversational, all the while keeping his eyes trained on the man. Beneath Cameryn's coat, Kyle's arm encircled her in an iron band, the blade of the knife perpendicular to her kidney.

The woman laughed and shoved her hip against the man, also laughing. They were only yards away now—the woman wore a perfume that smelled like cloves.

Once again Kyle dropped his voice so low that Cameryn could barely register his words. "If you draw attention to us in any way I will go to Gertrude Gorman's house with this knife. I know your mammaw's there."

With his FedEx cap once again on his head, he tilted the bill down as the couple closed the gap. Cameryn could feel its stiff rim against her cheekbone. "Two old ladies won't be much of a challenge for someone like me. So try to look normal and keep walking. You're shaking. Put a smile on that pretty face."

Step, step, step, Cameryn kept moving forward, which seemed impossible when her mind was frozen on what was left behind in the sheriff's office. Justin, dying. Justin, already dead. Her grandmother. The blade pressed against the wool sweater, slicing yarn. Nodding at the couple as they passed them, Cameryn looked at their faces, but they didn't even register her face, too intent on their own conversation.

"Perfect," Kyle crooned when they were past. He

propelled Cameryn down the county courthouse back stairway that led to a plowed parking lot. The building's door had not quite closed shut when Cameryn heard the woman scream, "Oh my God, is that blood?" and the man's cry, "It looks like footprints. Coming from there. . . ."

"Keep moving," Kyle hissed.

She stumbled as he pushed her toward a black Jeep; Kyle righted her and lifted her so that for a moment her feet dangled inches above the ground. He set her down next to the Jeep and opened the door.

"Get in."

Her muscles felt like wood. "No," she croaked. "If you're going to stab me, do it here." She knew the statistics; once a victim got into a car his or her life was basically over. It was better to take your chances on the outside. But Kyle, pushing the blade in so hard she cried out in pain, whispered, "Do what I tell you and your grandmother lives. Give me any trouble and I swear I will go to that house and slit her throat."

"Mammaw?" she gasped.

"Don't you get it? It's *you* I want. And now you've got a choice." His hazel eyes blazed. "Do you seriously want me to hurt anyone else? I killed Justin because of you. Do you want another soul on your conscience?"

She could barely get her mouth to move. "No."

"Good girl. Good Catholic girl. All the police are at

the Old Hundred Mine and there is no one in this stupid town to help you. So get into the Jeep, Cammie, or more people will die. Final warning."

Fear stabbed her as her mind worked through the decision that was now not a choice. Kyle, who had once told her he killed because it gave him a thrill to have power over life and death, held every card. There was no doubt he could kill Mammaw. Or anyone else he chose. Slowly, she folded herself into the bucket seat. He grabbed her right hand and placed her wrist on top of the metal grab bar installed over the glove compartment. From a pocket he produced a thin piece of plastic. The zip tie was threaded around the bar and her wrist so fast she barely registered his motion as he pulled one end of the plastic so tight it cut into her wrist. She cried out in pain but he ignored her.

"That should do it. Now you won't be going anywhere. That first time I used duct tape on you, but I'm proud to say I've improved my style. There's no way out of a zip tie." He walked toward the driver's side, his movements sinuous, like a large cat. Tall and well muscled, Kyle was far too big for her to overpower. In the seconds it took for him to make his way around the car she jerked against the zip tie with all her strength, but it did not give.

"When are you going to learn to stop fighting?" Kyle asked as he slid into the driver's seat. He was talking fast, his movements disjointed. Pulling off his FedEx cap he tossed it into the backseat. He set the knife on the dashboard and the Jeep's engine roared to life. Blood glazed the knife blade, and she thought of the red stained glass in St. Patrick's, the red frosting on her grandmother's Valentine cookies, and the red of her father's once fiery hair. Strange, disconnected thoughts, confetti memories whirling behind her eyes, useless memories of the ones she loved.

"Kyle, please," she whispered. "Please!"

"Please *what*?" He ran a hand through his hair then clasped the wheel. His posture was military, so straight the small of his back did not touch the upholstery. Blond hair stood from his head like an areola, longer than it had been when she'd last seen him. The features on his face seemed coarser, more hardened, his skin darkened by days lived in the open. With a lazy flick of his finger he turned on the blinker and coasted slowly out of the parking lot, stopping properly, checking the traffic in both directions before moving on at the proper speed. There was nothing about the two of them that would draw anyone's attention as he turned onto Greene Street.

"See, Cammie, last time, when I had you in my chicken coop, I didn't kill you. I walked away. I gave you a chance. But I won't do that again. This time it's just you and me and eternity."

Cameryn could feel her mouth widen in horror.

"See, the thing is, I'm tired of the game. I want to

end it but I want it to be memorable. So I'll take you with me. It will be poetic. Me and my *anam cara*."

"*Stop calling me that.*"

"I will call you whatever I want."

It was stupid to fight him, but she tried. If she was going to die it would not be passively sitting in the seat of a car. With her left arm flailing in a fist, she hit him as hard as she could, for Justin, for herself, and, for her mother and father and her mammaw. But he caught her fingers in his right hand and squeezed so hard she felt the bones crunch as she screamed in real pain.

"Don't do that, Cammie," he said coolly. "I'm driving and it's not safe. My, my, my, you are a hellcat, aren't you?"

"Let me *go!*" she said, swearing. Her fingers throbbed as he clamped down harder. And even though she didn't want to, she cried out again.

"That's not appropriate language from my *anam cara*." Dropping her hand, Kyle looked at her, his eyes amused. "The thing is, you're not in a position to tell me what to do, Cameryn Mahoney. You are my Angel of Death. And I own my angel."

What does that mean? Frantically, she searched for anyone who could help her. Her left hand, almost useless, could still signal someone's attention. In February, though, the plowed streets of Silverton were strangely empty, and the storefronts stood shuttered like pastel-colored ghosts. She searched for cars, trucks, pedestrians, anyone who might see her thrashing. Nothing. They might as well have been driving through a cemetery.

Moments later they left the buildings behind them and had reached the fork at the end of town. He carefully turned on his signal and headed north. Mountain peaks loomed above her, towering granite capped by a shimmering pearl white layer of snow. Overhead the blue sky mocked her. Spruce trees, dark green against the white, marched away from her up the mountainside, their legions a useless army. She struggled against the zip tie but it held her fast. Her heart was pounding, her breath coming in short gasps. The ends of her fingers were turning white as the strong plastic tie dug into her flesh and she thought of animals gnawing off their own limbs in order to be free. If she could, she would do it to free herself from this monster. But the knife was out of reach and there was nothing she could do.

Exultant, Kyle crowed, "Do you know how much preparation this took? Weeks of thinking. Weeks of planning." A strange smile twisted his almost perfect features, distorting them so that she wondered that she'd ever thought him handsome. "I knew you were lying to me the whole time. I knew they would make you say what you did. Cammie, I was outside your house the whole time, watching."

Through stone lips she whispered, "But you called me from Leather Ed's phone. . . ."

"No, I used a spoofcard. Mobile invisibility." He tapped the side of his head. "It's all about the technology. A spoofcard subverts the caller ID system." He spoke to her as though he had to make it simple enough for a child. "I turned on Leather Ed's cell phone and left it there at the mine. They've probably found the phone by now, but"—he frowned comically—"they won't find me."

"I. Don't. Care." She put a space between every word.

"But you should!" His golden eyebrows shot up on his forehead. "I'm probably the only one you know who's smarter than you. And now the game really begins."

Cameryn's mind raced. Feelings whirled around her head in a blur, but there was one sure bit of knowledge that sliced into her consciousness more clearly than the blade of Kyle's knife he'd thrust against her back. *He is going to kill me. Now, or very soon, my life will be over.* She should have known she was living on borrowed time and she thought of Justin and her grandmother, her mother and her father. Before, when he'd tied her up in his chicken coop, Kyle had told her he would return for her.

"Two guarantees," he'd said. "First, they'll never,

ever find me. And second"—he'd held up his middle and index fingers, pressing them together in a salute—"one day, when you least expect it, I'll be back."

Despite the barrier of her father's and Justin's protection, she was helpless once again. Fear rose in her like bile as Kyle downshifted, the Jeep now careening around deep bends more wildly. The needle on the speedometer inched up to sixty, then seventy, too fast for the winding mountain road.

You got out of it once, you can do it again. Don't give up! But what else had he said? As the trees streamed by, she searched her mind for a chink in his emotional armor, trying as hard as she could to bring up memories she'd forced beneath the veil of buried thoughts. *Think,* she commanded. *Think, think, think.* He'd told her that she was like him, an idea that made her recoil. But it was a thread she could follow. Desperate, she began, "You said, before, that we are the same. Tell me why you think that, Kyle." She barely squeezed out the words, but she knew it was best to keep him talking. To use his name.

"It won't work, Cammie," he answered, laughing coldly. "I read the same books. I know all about the psychology of a killer. You're trying to humanize yourself, aren't you? According to the books, though, there's something not quite right with my brain. I don't care if people die. Not even me. In fact, I'm going to welcome it."

Frantic, she cried, "You let me live because of my mother. I met Hannah, right before Christmas. I met her because of *you*. You let me live, Kyle. You did a good thing. Hannah's moved back to New York and she's great—we talk all the time. There's still good in you!"

He downshifted again, his foot pressing the gas pedal to the floor. "Did you tell her about me?"

"I didn't want to worry her. *Slow down!*" she screeched.

"Then I guess you didn't say a proper good-bye."

"Kyle, *why*—"

"Because I want people to remember me. I *told* you, Cammie, I've played the game and I keep winning. I'm bored. If I go out I want to take someone with me. There's a place called the Ruby Walls where the drop is a thousand feet straight onto rock. No guardrail to stop a car—nothing but air." His hand flew from the steering wheel, straight out until it touched the windshield's glass. "I thought you and me would sail right over the side and into eternity." He looked at her and smiled, flashing teeth. Kyle's face had frozen like a mask, everything dead, even his eyes. The flecks of gold in them had turned to ash.

"*No!*"

In reply he gunned the car faster, the engine whining as it made its final ascent. They crested the top and began the winding path down the narrow band of asphalt cut into the mountainside. Boulders covered by shrouds of snow whizzed past as Cameryn tensed, aware of things she'd never noticed before: the way her chest filled with air and the beat of her heart in her wrists, a heart whose beats were numbered. There had to be a way. To live and not die. The knife lay on the plastic dashboard, gleaming in its sheath of blood. Her left hand, crushed, almost useless. Not enough strength. Not enough time.

The plan came to her, and she realized she was putting the pieces together with surprising calmness. Thinking, calculating, she tugged on her collar with her throbbing left hand to help herself breathe. He was like a statue chiseled from the inside; the only thing left was a hollow shell of a human being. But maybe enough of a husk remained. With a deep, wavering breath, she looked at him. "Kyle," she said.

Her voice was almost drowned out by the drone of the engine.

"Kyle," she said again. "Look at me."

"What is it, Cameryn? Another game? We'll have forever now to play them."

She swallowed hard, trying by the sheer force of her will to keep her panic down so she could speak. It all came down to this. "Kyle, before you do it, before you drive off the pass, there's something you should know. . . ."

Chapter Sixteen

"YOU'RE LYING," KYLE said. "You want me to believe that there's something I should know." His words seemed to taunt her as he clutched the wheel so hard the vessels seemed to pop from beneath the skin of his hands.

Cameryn took a breath, trying to clear her mind in a wild bid to buy time. She could feel the seconds of her life were ticking away, each second, each heartbeat, each breath, almost her last. Fear rose and bloomed so large she could barely exhale. *Control,* she told herself. *Stay in control.*

"So what is it?" Kyle snorted with contempt. "Nothing, right? You're trying to buy some time. A pathetic attempt, Cammie. I expected better from my *anam cara.*"

When she couldn't answer, he said, "Yeah, that's what I thought. See, there's nothing you can do. I've already covered all the bases. Kyle O'Neil is calling the shots, just like always."

"No—I just don't know how to put what I'm thinking into words. *Please* slow down."

In reply, Kyle pushed the petal harder; the engine whined in protest as the trees streamed past in streaks of green.

"*Kyle!*"

"Relax, we're almost there." He leaned forward so that his chest brushed the steering wheel, his face manic, intent, his eyes narrowed to slits. "You can see into my mind by what I'll leave behind. You and me, crushed to pieces on the rocks below. I'm thinking the car might explode and then all they'll find will be ashes. Instant cremation. What a way to go."

"Don't—"

"Why not? I'm not afraid to die." A sadistic energy emanated from his erect body, and with one hand he gestured wildly. "*Everybody* dies, remember—mortality rate stands at one hundred percent. It's all about making a *statement*. Whoo!" He pumped his fist in the air. "*Yeah!*"

"Aren't you scared about what comes after?"

He glanced quickly at her, his eyes alight with a strange gleam. "You mean hell? If there is a hell,

I'm running it. I'm smarter than the devil, Cammie. Haven't you noticed that I never kill in a common way—man, I have a *signature*! Exotic deaths. They'll write about me *forever*, in their pointless little journals about the psychopathic mind. But like I said, I'm tired of playing. Now I just want to win. And I want to take you along for the ride." He made a *tsk*ing sound between his teeth. "Me an only child, and you raised all alone. Both of us are drawn to death and now we'll be going there together, sailing beyond straight into the other side. It's perfect."

"This doesn't have to end!" She was screaming now. Pleading with someone who didn't seem to feel, her words falling like petals against stone.

"Yes," he said calmly. "I think it does."

Outside she saw a meadow unfold before her, the tall stalks of yellow grass peeking out of the snow like the bristles of a golden brush. They were driving through the one last open expanse before the final descent into Ouray, to the sheer cliff of the Ruby Walls, the place where she and Kyle would die. Mount Abrams rose to the east: an amphitheater of rock touching the sky dome, void of trees, glistening as though it had been topped with pastillage.

He was going fast, much too fast, on this last straight stretch of road. Only moments to make a plan.

"Kyle, listen to me. No, just listen." There was desperation in her voice that she couldn't control. "Back in the cemetery, when you kissed me, something happened."

"Really." He gave her a strange half smile. "And what was it that happened to you, Cammie? What *feeling* did I unlock?"

"I think—I think it was the way that you said we both are drawn to death. But I don't think we need to die, Kyle." She placed her swollen left hand on his thigh. Her stomach roiled as she touched him, but she could see no other way than this. "I think we can both live. I *know* we can. We don't have to go off the mountainside. You and me—we can be together."

He laughed hollowly. "And how would that look to the outside world? Cameryn Mahoney and her little zip tie, following me around like a dog on a plastic leash. Or do you think no one would notice the binding?"

"No, Kyle." Her head whipped from the road to his face as she tugged against the plastic cord, helpless, trapped. Images, maybe the last she would ever see, streaked by, so much beauty in the colors that spun in a kaleidoscope of blues and greens, browns and every shade of white, this world she was not ready to leave. "I don't need this—*thing*. Cut me free and I'll show you. Kyle, I think you were right about us all along." Her breath was coming in gasps as she said, "You said you loved me."

He snorted. "But you don't love me. I already told you, I'm smarter than you are, even with that famous forensic brain of yours. You can't play with my mind, Cammie. I can see all of your moves."

The mountain was coming on fast.

"Kyle—*we belong together.* Why don't you—try to see if your life is worth living! Why die before you're sure?" The strangled words sounded so false she didn't dare to believe he would buy any of it. But something behind his eyes seemed to flicker. A pause. A tiny consideration.

"Kyle!"

"Stop saying my name. You're saying my name so I'll see you as a person. I know the tricks."

"I'm not trying to trick you." She was frantic now—ready to promise him anything if he would just put his foot on the brake. "I mean it. I *swear!*"

Thrusting out his jaw, he stared straight ahead. "So you think you have . . . feelings . . . for me." There was an almost imperceptible change in his tone. Some of the arrogance has gone, replaced by something akin to sadness.

The chink hold was all she needed. "I *know* I do."

"You said you cared for me. On the phone. You said you'd be there if I gave myself up, but it wasn't true."

"That's because they *made* me say that. I wanted to go but they wouldn't let me."

"The police . . ."

"They told me what I had to do. *They* wrote down the words and they were standing right there. What would you have done?"

"I wouldn't have lied to you. You and me—I let you live, and then you turned against me."

Cameryn almost laughed at the absurdity of his words. He wouldn't lie to her, but he would kill her in a murder-suicide, send them sailing over the side of the mountain to certain and irrevocable death. But she couldn't let her mind even register anything more than the toehold she'd gained. With a wavering breath she said, "Let me prove it to you. There's a pull-off coming up. Take it, Kyle. Turn in and stop the car."

"I don't think I can do that."

They were racing toward the mountain. The tall peak cast its shadow onto the meadow, turning the snow a shimmering blue in the half-light and then, too fast, the shadow swallowed them whole. And then they were there. The mountain loomed above them and the switchback road with its sheer, unprotected drop began. To her left, an ever-deepening chasm. To her right, an unyielding wall of granite.

"It's up ahead. Pull over! Please, please, just give me one minute! *Please*, Kyle!"

"Why?"

"Let me prove it to you!"

The vertical stone loomed above her so expansively she could no longer see the sky. If her hand had been free she could have reached out and touched it. Years ago miles of rock had been jackhammered away to create the thinnest precipice, a thread of asphalt more dangerous than any other highway in Colorado.

Kyle's voice was suddenly low. "How can I believe you?"

This was it. Closing her eyes, she said, "Because you were right all along. You knew me better than I knew myself. And we don't have to die. You are my *anam cara*."

"I am?"

"Yes."

"You wouldn't lie to me?"

"No."

And then, miraculously, the car began to slow. She opened her eyes to watch as he removed his foot from the gas pedal. Centrifugal force propelled them, the Jeep's tires squealing as he made one hairpin turn, but his foot, hesitant at first, moved to the left to gently press upon the brake. The smallest of hesitations that could mean her life.

Not daring to speak, she waited, frozen, aware anything else she said now might be wrong. She knew this road. Three turns ahead lay the pullout, her sliver of hope.

Ten seconds later there it was—the crescent carved into the mountain, big enough for a single vehicle. She didn't blink. She did not dare to blink, to break the spell of the slowing car.

And then, as if even he didn't know what his body was doing, Kyle pulled the steering wheel and slammed on the brakes, skidding into the snow until they stopped in a movement so sudden Cameryn felt her neck lash forward and then back. In the silence she could hear them both panting as Kyle turned toward her.

"I must be stupid to listen, but maybe . . . show me," he said.

"I will."

To the left the mountain sheered down in a drop-off guaranteed to kill. To the right, the stone wall, varnished in a layer of ice, seeming to reach into eternity. She couldn't see beyond the bend. Her prayer had been that a car or truck, any vehicle would appear, but the traffic was sparse in the winter over this pass and the two of them were utterly alone. In the abstract her idea made sense; but Kyle was looking at her in a way that engendered a new kind of fear. And then the thought that crystallized inside her: what would she do to save her life?

This. I can do this. As she moved close to him, he grabbed the back of her head and pressed her mouth violently into his. Like a statue she held herself immobile, her fists constricting as she forced herself to stay still. Compliant. He was working himself up, more brutal now. She could feel the anger in him, the rage as his tongue barged into her mouth.

"Is this what you mean?" he asked hoarsely. "Because if you can love me, I will let you live. I'll let *us* live." Wrapping her hair around his forearm, he yanked her face to him so hard that her right arm twisted in its socket. She gasped in pain.

"Do you love me, Cammie?"

He forced her to look into his hazel eyes. The gold was back, shimmering like flakes of metal against warm wood. Wide-set, they pleaded with her, the eyes of a manic child.

"Yes," she answered, as gently as she could. "Yes, Kyle, I do."

"Then show me again."

This time his hands were soft on her face. These were the hands that killed Justin. This body, this inhuman being she had to pretend to care for, leaned into her and pressed his lips against hers. Repulsed, she issued orders to her body, signals from the general of her mind to the soldiers that made up the parts of her. She commanded her mouth to follow his, her arms to flex toward him, not away. As he kissed her, she felt her mind detach from her body, separate and hover somewhere above them near the ceiling of the car.

A lone car roared by, then vanished beyond the bend, useless to her. Finally, he pulled back and sighed contentedly. "*That's* what I remember," he said.

"Yes." It was all she could manage to say.

"You can see into me and see something worth saving."

"I can."

He moved close and put his arms around her, a lover's embrace with no hint of violence. Gently, he put his lips to her ear and whispered, "The thing is, I'm not stupid, Cammie. I know you are lying to me. But I give you credit for trying. It was a good effort. Really, really good. A kiss before dying."

And then in one fluid motion he sat back and floored the gas pedal, the Jeep fishtailing as it reentered the Million Dollar Highway.

But she was still close to him, just as she had planned to be. Beneath her, the gearshift knob rose like a beacon, only inches away, as the speedometer shot to thirty, thirty-five. *Now!* she screamed in her head. With all the strength she had left in her throbbing left hand she grabbed the ball of the knob, yanking it into reverse. Instantly the engine seized up with a violent spasm, the gears grinding in an almost human scream.

"What the—" Kyle swore in a fury as he wrenched

back into his seat. His strike was fast and hard. Balling his hand into a fist, he punched Cameryn in her cheek as the Jeep lurched into the other traffic lane. Bright lights shimmered behind her eyes as she held onto the gearshift, but the second punch sent her reeling and Kyle once again took control of the gearshift.

He swore again as he tried to reset the gear, his attention solely on the car.

It was the millisecond Cameryn had planned on, had prayed for. As his hand clutched the knob, Cameryn grasped the steering wheel and pulled to the right with every ounce of strength she had. Her elbow snapped as he broke her hold but it was too late; the Jeep pitched toward the mountain. A sickening squeal of metal against rock as the front end of the Jeep collided with granite. Sparks shot out like the end of a sparkler and then there was an explosion so loud it felt like a gunshot had ripped through her head. The breath knocked out of her as she whipped back into the seat, and then . . . silence.

Smoke clouded the interior of the Jeep, stinging her lungs. She heard coughing and a quiet moan from Kyle. Deflated airbags hung down like white curtains as she blinked, trying to right herself again. Through the cracked windshield she saw the car had come to rest at a ninety-degree angle against the mountain. The car's hood had crumpled into pleats.

Kyle was not moving. She saw there were smudges of

smoke smeared across his face like war paint, and his hands hung limp in his lap. And then she saw what she was looking for: the knife. It had skidded forward, at the edge of the dashboard, just within reach. She could cut herself free with its blade. Her left hand, swollen and bruised, pulsed with every beat of her heart, but she forced herself to go slowly, to reach past Kyle. Her fingers stretching, the blade, still red with Justin's blood, glancing against her fingertips, and then pain exploding against her hand.

"I'll take that," he said, plucking the knife by the handle.

She could see the cold rage in his eyes as he kicked his way out the driver's door, the knife clutched in his hand. In a flash he was at the passenger side; there was enough space for him to yank open her door, the hinges groaning in protest. The blade winked in the light.

The sharp edge whipped up over her head and she watched its arc, sure of where it would strike. Her heart. It was aimed at her heart.

She saw her parents and Justin and her school, Lyric, and her life, a shaken snow globe of memories. But the blade did not slice into her chest as she expected. Instead, she felt a stab as the knife cut against the zip tie that held her wrist to the grab bar. She was free. Mercifully free.

Tossing the knife in the air, he caught it with his

left as he yanked her out of the car, onto her knees. "Bitch," he spat. "We're going over the side, one way or another."

Her death had been postponed, but it was coming, just the same.

Screaming, kicking, she tried to hold on but she was no match for him and his strength as he pulled her across the Million Dollar Highway.

"No!" she cried, but he did not hear her. She dug her heels into the slick asphalt but there was nothing to brace her, no way to stop him. His grip around her wrist was like a vise. He grunted as he pulled her into the center, halfway across the line, then five feet from the edge. From there she caught a flash of the bottom, the sheer drop that ended in juts of stone so ragged they looked like teeth. There was no way to live through a fall like that. Her chances would have been better protected by the steel of the Jeep.

"Oh God, don't do this!" she begged.

"God's not doing it," he said, leering. "I am."

And then, like a miracle from heaven, she heard a rumble from below. A semi appeared around the bend, blowing black smoke from an upright exhaust pipe. The driver looked down as the blue cab roared toward them. In that moment when Kyle wavered, she acted. Twisting her arm against the joint where his thumb met his fingers, she broke his grasp. Staggering, she stepped backward while Kyle stared at the approaching truck, paralyzed with indecision.

The rear wheels of the cab smoked as it squealed then stopped less than ten feet away. The driver jumped to the ground, landing hard. He was thickly muscled, with a black mustache that brushed the edge of his jaw and a red plaid shirt.

"You all right?" the truck driver cried. "That's a bad wreck. You kids okay?" He held up a cell phone. "I already hit 911. They'll be here any moment." And then, as if he sensed something was off, the driver asked again, "You sure you're okay?" Then he saw the knife.

It seemed to take only a moment for Kyle to decide.

Backing up, he kept his eyes locked on hers as he took three long steps toward the lip of the road.

"Kid, what do you think you're doin'?" the trucker roared. He was running toward Kyle but Kyle stood tall, like a diver ready to make a back flip off an Olympic high dive.

"Kid!"

Kyle's arms flew out straight from his sides so that his body made the shape of the cross.

"I guess I'll make this last journey alone. Good-bye, Cammie. Make sure they write about me."

Then, without another word, he sailed backward, his eyes on Cameryn's as he arced into the air to disappear onto the rocks below.

Chapter Seventeen

THE BALLOONS IN her hand bobbed and swayed, looking like giant moons. While Cameryn rode up in the elevator she felt a similar lightness inside herself, as though she would rise up and touch the ceiling of Mercy Hospital. She was that happy.

The elevator *ding*ed, the doors slid open, and she made her way into the lobby of the third floor.

"Oh, those are nice," said the nurse at the station, whose name tag read *Betty*. "Who are you visiting?"

"Dr. Moore," she answered. "But these balloons aren't for him. Can I leave them here with you?"

"Certainly, dear. They're lovely. So nice and cheerful!"

"Thanks." Cameryn smiled back. "Dr. Moore's present is in my backpack," she said, twisting around as though the nurse could see.

Betty said, "So you're here delivering *two* presents.

Aren't you an angel." The woman was in her sixties, with crepey skin that held too much rouge and hair dyed the color of a Halloween pumpkin. But her tone was sweet, and as Cameryn walked down the hallway she heard the balloons gently tapping each other.

The room wasn't far away. Knocking softly, Cameryn stepped inside the small enclosure. A striped curtain had been pulled back, and she saw the doctor, propped on a hospital bed that was nearly flat. Tufts of white hair encircled his head like a fallen halo. His nose looked swollen, his skin pale. She was about to back out of the room so she wouldn't disturb him when she saw his eyes flutter open.

"Miss Mahoney," he said, his voice weak. "My protégée."

"Hi, Dr. Moore. How are you feeling today?"

"Sore." He pressed a button that raised the bed until he was almost sitting. "A bit fuzzy from the meds. But grateful the cancer was contained, which I think I told you when you came by yesterday. You were here yesterday, correct? Or was I dreaming?"

She set the backpack just inside the door. "Yes, I was here. This is my third day visiting."

"Uh-huh, that's right." He nodded. "If all goes well I'll be up and running in a little over six weeks, which means we'll be back on deck, with me at the helm. I'd like to hire you to work for me while you're at Fort Lewis College. Did I ask you that already?"

"You did," she answered, smiling. "And I said yes."

"Good! You'll be right up the street from me in the dorms. Are you amenable to working for a cantankerous old coot instead of a nice, calm coroner like your father?"

"It depends on how much you're willing to pay me," Cameryn said, laughing, relieved that the fog seemed to be lifting from the doctor's mind. "I'd like to confirm a number while you're under the influence of narcotics," she told him. "To take full advantage of the situation."

He waved her words away as though he were fanning gnats. "My point is there's still a lot I need to teach you, Miss Mahoney. Sit."

"I can only stay a minute, Dr. Moore. I have someone else I need to see."

"This will only take a minute. Take that chair. Yes, pull it closer."

Cameryn dragged a green fabric chair with metal legs close to the side of his bed, the legs screeching against the linoleum floor, and sat down.

The doctor picked up his glasses from the bedside table and peered at her, his eyes too large behind the lenses. Reaching for a glass, he sipped water from a straw, then carefully set it down again. His fingers trembled as he adjusted the folds of his sheets, pressing them into furrows until they looked like a miniature field ready for planting. Clearing his throat, he began, "I'm a sick old man who wants to give you some advice. Will you listen?"

Cameryn hesitated. Even though he didn't seem to remember her visit the day before, this conversation threatened to take essentially the same form. She braced herself for what she knew was coming.

"Miss Mahoney, it's easy at your age to get side-tracked by love."

"Dr. Moore—" she began to protest, but the doctor talked right over her.

"I know, you think I'm too ancient to remember what it's like to be young. But my great age brings wisdom, and that wisdom compels me to remind you that what you have is a gift." He winced as he adjusted himself to face her. "No matter what, you need to stay the course with your career in medicine. Listen to an old sage. I've been around a long time—maybe too long—but I have been privileged to meet the best future forensic pathologist the field will produce. You!"

"I think that's just the drugs talking," she answered, shifting uncomfortably in her seat.

"This isn't codeine, Miss Mahoney—I'm on half the meds I was yesterday because I want to get my mind clear."

"You do sound better," she admitted.

"I've been lying in this bed, thinking. I'm a patient who just dodged a cancer bullet, who will live to work and teach another day."

"Which is so great—"

"And this amazing young woman is the one I want to pour my knowledge into, teaching her every trick I know." He fingered a plastic tube that had been taped to the back of his hand. Sounding wistful, he said, "I have tricks . . . well, *techniques* might be a better word. But what you have is brilliance." He tapped the side of his head, causing the tubing to dance across the sheets. "You got yourself out of a jam with that Kyle O'Neil by thinking. That kind of intelligent tenacity is hard to come by."

"My mammaw calls it stubbornness," Cameryn replied as she raised an eyebrow.

He chuckled, pressing the button again to raise himself even farther; the machinery hummed until he stopped at a forty-five-degree angle. "Stubbornness is one facet of your personality, certainly. I like it, if you want to know the truth. But you're so young. Life comes at you hard when you're seventeen."

"Eighteen. I'm eighteen today."

"Congratulations and happy birthday. Life comes at you even harder when you're eighteen." He winked, then hesitated, and Cameryn began to wonder if that was all he was going to say, but he trained his blue eyes on hers. "Do you remember what the word *autopsy* means?"

Cameryn nodded. "It means 'to see with one's own eyes.'"

"Precisely." He dropped his chin into his bullfrog neck and peered at her over the rims of his glasses. "With *my* eyes I'm seeing what you will be if you keep your hand on the rudder. Don't turn away from your future. An artist isn't an artist if she doesn't paint."

She thought about this. Today, on her birthday, she had chosen to wear her Mahoney sweater again, even though it was the clothing she'd almost died in. But as she'd reached into her closet in the morning she'd decided it was more than that. It had been knitted with the luck of the Irish, her perfect birthday cloth—the sweater she'd *stayed alive* in. Kyle O'Neil's crumpled body lay in the Montrose morgue, while Cameryn was in a hospital with those she cared for, truly ready for the first time in her life for whatever would come. Her future lay wide open, vast with promise, but the new became possible only because of what had taken place before. Facing her own death had made her see that life was a series of threads as intertwined as the Aran yarn. Yet it seemed impossible to express what she'd learned. She sat quiet, thinking there was no way to wrap this knowledge into words.

"Are you going to tell me that I'm an old geezer who needs to butt out?"

"No." Leaning forward so that her elbows drilled her knees, she said, "Do you remember the fortune cookie that predicted your future?"

He looked at her quizzically. "Yes, I remember sharing that story with you. About the whimsical fortune cookie that pointed me to my life with the dead—the one that showed me which medical path to pursue. It led me to the dark art of forensics."

"Yeah, that's the one. The fortune said *You will touch the hearts of many.* Remember? And you figured it meant you would go into forensic pathology so you could touch a lot of hearts of decedents when you preformed autopsies."

"I'm pleased you were listening."

Equally intense, Cameryn told him, "I've decided that I can also touch the hearts of many—dead people, but the living, too."

He waited a beat before saying, "The living?"

"Yes, the living. You don't have to choose one or the other, Dr. Moore. I realized this when I thought I might be going over the side of a cliff, as dramatic as that sounds. I don't think it would have been forensics that I would have missed, but the people that I love. They were the ones I was fighting to get back to. The living, Dr. Moore, not the dead."

Shaking his head grimly, he said, "You sound so young."

"And you're sounding tired so I'm going to let you rest. I promise I'll keep up my work and be a good student and do everything you want, but I'm going to do everything *I* want, too. That's what's so cool about being eighteen," she said, rising to her feet. "I can dream big." She paused. "Oh, I brought this for you."

She opened her backpack and pulled out a book, setting it into the doctor's hands.

"What's this?"

"An art book. It's called *The Last Rose of Summer* by Robert McGinnis. It's to make your wife happy. The grass you painted is beautiful, but don't forget to put in the flowers, too. That's where the color is. Now *I'm* sounding like a fortune cookie." She leaned over to squeeze his hand before slipping out of the room, sure she could hear the sound of a faint chuckle as the door clicked shut.

Back at the nurses' station she picked up her dozen balloons from Betty, who was chatting with a male nurse in blue scrubs.

"That's the angel I was telling you about," Betty said, while Cameryn disappeared into the elevator, catching her image in the shiny steel doors. The fuzzy reflection seemed older, more confident. The balloons bobbed against the ceiling as she exited onto the fourth floor, her heart skipping as she approached the room.

Forensics had taught her that scars left tissue much tougher than skin. In a way she was stronger now, and so was he. Stronger together than they ever would be apart.

This time she didn't knock but instead opened the

door quietly. Justin was sleeping, his chest rising and falling gently, his head bent to one side, his dark hair tousled against the pillow. For a moment she stood there, watching. A machine beeped in the background while light poured into the room in pale yellow squares. One knee propped the sheets into a tent. He must have sensed she was there because he stirred.

"Cammie," he murmured. It was barely a whisper, caught between wakefulness and sleep.

"I'm here," she answered, as she stepped forward into their new life.

Acknowledgments

I'd like to thank the many people who helped me explore the forensic field. You have unselfishly shared your knowledge and passion—the glimpse into your world rocked mine! I'm especially grateful to: Thomas M. Canfield, MD, Fellow at the American Academy of Forensic Sciences, Chief Medical Examiner, Office of Medical Investigations; Kristina Maxfield, Coroner; Robert C. Bux, MD, Coroner, Medical Examiner, Forensic Pathologist; David L. Bowerman, Coroner, Forensic Pathologist; Dawn Miller, Deputy Coroner; Werner Jenkins, Chief Forensic Toxicologist; Chris Clarke, Forensic Toxicologist; Sandy Way, Administrator, El Paso County Coroner's Office; Sheriff Sue Kurtz, San Juan County Sheriff's Office; Melody Skinner, Administrative Assistant, San Juan County Sheriff's Office; Chief Michael J. Phibbs, Elizabeth Police Department; Thomas Carr, Archeologist, Colorado Historical Society; and a special thanks to Robert Scott Mackey, D-ABMDI Deputy Coroner and Chris Herndon, Deputy Coroner, El Paso County Coroner's Office—two inspiriting professionals and my conduits into a macabre world.

Alane Ferguson is the author of *The Christopher Killer,* an Edgar Award Nominee, *The Angel of Death*, and *The Circle of Blood*—three previous books about Cameryn Mahoney. She does intensive research for her books, attending autopsies and interviewing forensic pathologists as she delves into the fascinating world of medical examiners.

Ms. Ferguson lives with her family near the foothills of the Colorado Rockies. For more information about the author and her books, please visit **www.alaneferguson.com**.